Black Ink Publications Presents

Killa

Chronicles of a Killer

A Novel by

Sa'id Salaam

**Email: saidmsalaam@gmail.com and/or
blackinkpublications1@gmail.com
Facebook: Free Sa'id Salaam
Cover design and layout by:
Edited by:**

Acknowledgments

Bismillah Ir Rahman Ir Raheem
As always, First and Foremost All praise and worship is
for Almighty God, alone, with no partners. I bear witness that
there is nothing worthy of worship except Him.

Killa

Chronicles of a Killer

A Novel by

Sa'id Salaam

Prologue

The doctor looked at his patient skeptically as he set the parameters into his laptop. The program was designed to monitor stress in the voice, as well as excitement, pauses, stutters and stammers. In short, it was a super lie detector. Emotion indicating faces (happy, sad, etc.) accompanied the meters.

It required no wires or cameras, nothing but normal conversation. As he worked, he made congenial small talk with the young shackled man before him. The doctor was paid to be skeptical, but the more he looked at the slight soft-spoken subject the more he doubted what he read in the patient's file.

"Doesn't look so tough to me," the doctor thought to himself. "I probably could take him myself," he laughed, but still shot a comforting glance at the door where a sheriff's deputy was posted.

"Officer, we're ready to begin," he instructed the bored deputy.

"You sure you wanna be left alone with this one," the sheriff offered, half-heartedly, already reaching for the handle.

"Yes, doctor/patient privilege and all that," he replied. "Plus Xavier and I are good buddies.

Xavier discreetly flexed against his restraints as he smiled agreeing, "Sure we are doc."

With that the deputy shot out the door in search of the cute nurse he spied on the way in.

"So what do you like to be called Xavier, X or do you have a nickname?"

"Yeah Killa. Everyone calls me Killa."

"Killer?" the doctor asked incredulously. He was mildly shocked that facing the charges ahead of him that he would use that particular moniker.

"Killa it is," he said pressing the space bar on the laptop, starting the recording. "Okay Killa, let's start at the beginning. Tell me about your first kill."

Chapter 1

"Hmmm my first time," Killa exhaled as if recalling a fond memory. The doctor furrowed his brow as the machine's meters that indicated pleasure.

"I had to be like four, yeah four, just before my fifth birthday. I remember because we had went school shopping that day. I was starting kindergarten soon, P.S. 129."

"P.S.? Public school?" The doctor inquired unfamiliar with the term.

"Yeah that's how most elementary schools are named in New York, middle schools too. I think only high schools are named. Named after white people of course Taft, Walton, Clinton, anyway..."

"I'm from University Homes, the projects. Highbridge section of the Bronx," Killa said as the meters still indicated pleasure.

"What kind of area is that?" the doctor asked.

"Oh, it's the hood," Killa said emphatically, "shootouts, stickups, hood shit."

"Figures," the doctor thought inwardly. So many of the patients referred to him recalled similar upbringings. Projects, crack addicted parents, violence at developmental stages, no fathers *hood shit indeed* registered sarcasm.

"Was your dad around," he asked expecting a negative reply.

"Yeah pops was around 'til he got killed," Killa replied meters indicating stress.

"Murdered? Your dad was murdered?" the doctor asked hoping to expound on the stress registering on the screen.

"Yup, that was when I got my first kill," Killa replied.

"Wait! You killed your dad?" the doctor exclaimed.

"Fuck naw nigga, I ain't kill my pops," Killa exploded sending the meters into the red. The doctor shivered inwardly at the display of emotion. Now the baby faced thirty-year-old in front of him looked like a killer with the deadly glint in his eyes.

I'm sorry, please continue," the doctor said soothingly.

"Aight, yo me and my pops was mad close," Killa said as the meters indicated he was becoming calm again. "He ain't live with us, matter fact I found out later dude had a wife and more kids uptown. Ma Dukes was like the chick on the side.

Still my father was always around. See my dad was a hustler. He had my projects on lock. He used to keep work at the chicks' he was boning apartments. I guess that's how I got here.

They was always beefing yo. My moms yo, she would be stressing the hell out of him. Just fucking yelling and cursing 'til he bounced. I hated her for that shit. Word up son, pops will come to check a nigga and this bi... this chick would run him off."

"Typical," the doctor thought to himself. A lot of men had love/hate relationships with their moms. This was at the high range of hate so the meters said. If his chart didn't say his

Sa'id Salaam

mother committed suicide he would have thought he killed her himself.

"Yeah the day my pops died he came through, had me a pair of new J's. My father bought me every pair of Jordans that came out. Dude was plugged in, so I had 'em first. That's how I got my Jordan fetish, from my pops."

The doctor smiled along with his client and the machine indicating pleasure.

"Anyway, as usual she starts beefing with the nigga about him not leaving any work and..." Killa went on as the scene played in his head.

"Bitch, you done fucked up four ounces. No way in the fuck I believe that bullshit 'you lost it'", Killa's father boomed *as he tossed the bedroom in search of the drugs. "Every time I leave some work here shit come up short," he said as their child listened from the hallway.*

"What the fuck you doing?" Killa's mother screamed as he opened her top drawer. "Get out of my shit," she said pulling him away from the dresser.

"Un huh, is this what you tryna hide?" he yelled holding up a crack pipe. "Is this why my money short?" he asked punctuating the query with a vicious back hand.

"Gimme my pipe!" Killa's mother screamed unfazed by the hard slap.

"Bitch, I ain't giving you shit!" he yelled pushing her away. "Look at this," he said retrieving rocks of cocaine from the drawer.

7

"Gimmeeeeee!!" she screamed hysterically as she tried to recover her drug.

"I'm throwing this shit out," he said heading out the room.

The sight of her drugs being taken away was more than the addict could take. She scrambled to her bed and pulled a .38 caliber pistol from the mattress. Just as Killa's father passed him in the hallway, the first shot spun him around. He locked eyes with his shocked son for an instant before the next shot slammed him against the wall.

He looked at the hole in his chest, then to the woman holding the smoking revolver. "That's that bullshit," he groaned and slid down the wall.

"Oh my God," his mother screamed coming to grips with what she did. "I'm sorry baby," she said rushing to his aid. She sat the pistol down and tried to help the dead man. "Uh uh, baby, don't go to sleep, you gonna be okay," she said in a panic.

"Then what happened?" the doctor asked snapping Killa from his silence.

"My bad," he said realizing he'd zoned out and stopped talking.

"I had a whachamacallit? An outer body experience," he explained.

"How so?" the doctor urged while monitoring the machine's meters. They showed nothing, zero emotion, as he replayed the events.

"I mean I did it, but it was like I didn't do it. Like I watched myself do it," he explained.

"Did what X… uh Killa, what did you do?" the doctor asked soothingly.

"I watched me pick up the gun and put it to my mother's head, then I pulled the trigger. I put the gown down then rejoined myself," he said, meters showing nothing.

"Then what happened?" the doctor asked urgently. He would have to reread the file after the session ended.

"Shit, I went and watched cartoons until the cops came. My grandmother lived in the next building so she came and got me. I guess they figured it to be a murder suicide cuz no one ever said nothing, so I ain't never say nothing…until now."

"Well, okay, Killa," the doctor said dubiously. "That's our time for today."

He of course didn't believe a word of the story. He had the official report on his parents' deaths. The mother was on drugs and the father was a known dealer, but the incident was, according to reports, a murder suicide.

Still the state of the lie detector showed no signs of deception. It did show some inappropriate emotions when he spoke of shooting his mother, but was dead on with elation when speaking of his dad. He clearly loved his father, and had disdain for his mother.

"The man is full of shit," the doctor surmised. "Trying to play crazy to avoid lethal injection," the doctor said to himself as the sheriff's deputy escorted his prisoner back to the high max section of the jail, the doctor set new parameters in his machine.

He used the presets for him and his wife that he'd set up unbeknownst to her. Using the speaker phone he dialed his wife's office to cancel their dinner plans.

After being screened by his wife's secretary who now knew his voice, yet still asked "Whom shall I say is speaking?" His call was put on a brief hold.

The doctor smiled in satisfaction at fighting the urge to curse her out for the umpteenth time.

"Hey dear, I'm very busy, do you need something?" his wife asked, exacerbation in her tone.

"Fine, honey, thanks. I need to beg off dinner this evening," he said without a trace of the intended sarcasm.

"That's fine dear, I need to do the same actually. Something's come up at the office," she said quickly, determined to spend as little time speaking with her husband as possible.

"Likewise, I got a ton of work dropped on me and…"

"Well, okay, dear. I'll see you at home," she said cutting him off.

If she said goodbye before hanging up the doctor missed it.

"Thing's working fine," the doctor said noticing that the program picked up both of their lies. The something that "came up" at the office was probably some guy's cock, and he had plans on seeing Xing Lee at the massage parlor.

Xing offered none of the drama that his wife shoveled at him daily. No bitching, no complaining just good loving. The doctor smiled rubbing his hands together in anticipation. Besides, can't complain when your mouth is full.

The doc glanced back over his session's notes.

"That... nah," the doctor said dismissing the thought that Killa's story was true. "No fucking way."

11

Chapter 2

A week later...

"You need me to stick around, Doc," the deputy asked as he settled Killa into his chair. His body language made it clear he was eager to go chase some nurses.

"No, we're fine aren't we Killa," the doctor replied optimistically.

"We good," Killa said plainly. The deputy shot out the door in a flash.

"So how was your weekend," the doctor asked by way of small talk. He wanted to recalibrate his program to ensure he got a good reading this time.

"Son ... I'm in a fucking eight by twelve concrete and steel cell with no windows... how the fuck you think my weekend went?" Killa answered curtly.

The doctor nodded with pleasure as the meters were in sync with the aggravation in his voice. "I'm sorry. I guess that was a rather insensitive question given your current living arrangement."

"I guess that's your way of saying *my bad*," Killa chuckled.

"Yes, my bad ... bro", the doctor chuckled holding up his fist in the Black power salute. He noted that Killa's amusement registered just as it should.

"Okay then, shall we begin?"

"Let's," Killa said mocking the doctor's prim demeanor.

"I'm curious," the doctor began tentatively, "tell me about your upbringing, your 'hood', do you think you've become a product of your environment?"

"No doubt. I mean how could I not?" Killa replied enthusiastically. "Don't get me wrong we produce other products than just killers or criminals. Doctors, lawyers, all kinda people come from the hood."

"So, what happened with you?" He asked sincerely.

"Shit, I just liked that hood shit, loved that shit, the guns, stacks of cash, even, even... shit I even like busting my gun," Killa said.

"You saw a lot of violence in your home?" he asked.

"In my house? Naw, I stayed with my grandmother. Just the two of us. She never even spanked me, but my projects were buck wild. Niggas getting shot, stabbed, the whole nine. I seen hoes sucking dick and fuckin' in the stairwell when I was like five or six. Shit I remember one time a nigga got hit up..."

"Killed? A nig... a-a-a person was killed?" the doctor asked obviously unfamiliar with the term 'hit up'.

"Pardon my vernacular," Killa chuckled lighting up the meters on the screen. "Yeah killed, murked, wet up, shot, knocked off. So I remember we heard shots that night but shit, that's everyday 'round my projects so we ain't think nothing of it. So, me and grandma we going shopping or some shit and as usual the elevator is broke so we hit the steps. Soon as we exit the stairwell dude is stretched the fuck out, eyes open."

"What was your grandmother's reaction? Was she startled? Did she scream?" the doctor asked fascinated.

"Sheeet ole gal been in dem projects thirty years. She was used to that shit. Stepped right over him – LOL- stepped over him like a puddle, then helped me over. She acted like it was nothing. When we got in later that day dude was still there. Them old church ladies was downstairs bitching like *they need to get that motherfucker off the steps; shit was crazy.*

"How long did he stay before the authorities came?" the doctor asked incredulously.

"That nigga was there until the next day. We had to step over him again to go to church in the morning. Shit was so casual, so ordinary, I really ain't think nothing of it. It wasn't until I actually saw a nigga get his shit twisted that, oh 'scuse me 'getting ya shit twisted' means getting killed," he said apologetically.

"Yeah I caught that one. I'm learning," the doctor laughed. "So tell me about that. Was that impactful?"

"Yeah that shit turned me out, yo," Killa said matter of factly, however the program was registering elation. The doctor frowned curiously as he went on.

"Yeah me and my lil man, Rico, had just started first grade; six years old. We used to walk to and from school together. Son's mom was a crack head so he would be at our

15

spot all the time. G-ma be feeding him and shit. So anyway, one day we get to our building and...

As Rico and Killa enter the building an older cat everyone called Tay was chastising Lil J about selling crack in the projects. Tay and a couple of other old heads claimed the exclusive rights to slang rocks in University Homes.

Although Tay and his counterparts were only in their early twenties, so to fifteen-year-old Lil J him and his crew were grown ass men.

"Man, I done told y'all lil niggas 'bout fucking with my money," Tay said jabbing the teenager in the chest with a finger as he spoke.

"We tryna eat too," Lil J whined, flinching but not scared.

"Take that shit over on Ogden Ave. or Nelson but we own this shit!" Tay screamed in his face.

Rico and Killa stood in the doorway as the exchange heated up. "Matter fact," Tay said as he began to go in J's pockets, "all that dough y'all made belong to me." He removed a sizable roll of cash from each of Lil J's front pockets.

"Don't take my money," Lil J pleaded as Tay turned to walk away.

"See, that's how you check a nigga," Tay bragged to Killa.

"Treat a hoe like a hoe," he told Rico before spinning around and slapping the taste out of Lil J's mouth. Literally as the Now & Later he'd been savoring flew across the lobby.

"Nawmean," Tay laughed as he turned to leave.

Rico was watching Tay, but Killa had his eyes on Lil J. He saw the kids eyes turn to stone as he reached into his waistband. He could take the chump off, could stand the loss of the day's earnings, hell he knew he was stepping on toes shortstopping traffic, but no one touches you, and to slap a dude is worse than punching him, worse than being spit on. It's the ultimate diss. Killa's eyes grew large as the chrome .380 appeared in Lil J's hand.

Tay saw Killa's reaction and wheeled around just in time to catch a slug between his eyes. A small spray of blood flew towards Rico and Killa as the impact jerked Tay's head back. Rico let out a high pitched shriek and took off up the stairs.

"A-yo who da bitch now?" Lil J laughed as he removed his money from Tay's dead hands. As he began rumbling through his pockets, Killa drew near. He squatted down to get a closer look at the dead eyes.

"You see who shot dis nigga?" Lil J asked cautiously.

"Shot who?" Killa responded, already hip to the game at six.

"My nigga," Lil J laughed handing him a bloody twenty dollar bill. "Now get outta here."

Lil J took off out the door, but Killa was stuck. He stayed there kneeled in front of the dead man as his blood pooled around him. By the time Killa regained his senses, he was in the middle of a pool of blood.

He slipped as he ran to the stairs but stayed upright. He left a trail of bloody Jordan prints up the stairs.

17

"Then what?" the doctor asked.

"Then him and the rest of them young niggas waited until the cops came and stood around in the crowd with the rest of the spectators. Keeps niggas from snitching."

"I bet," the doctor said astonished. "Well that's a wrap for today. I'll see you tomorrow – wait tomorrow's Saturday, see you Monday."

"Cool," Killa said calmly, "be easy."

Chapter 3

When Monday rolled around, Killa was back in the office to continue his psychiatric evaluation. He was ordered by the court to see if he was competent to stand trial.

His court appointed lawyer reasoned an insanity defense was the only way to keep a needle out of his client's arm. Truth be told, his lawyer assumed Killa was crazy. He'd been a crime buff his whole life and was familiar with serial killers. He had books on John Wayne Gacy, Ellen Wuornos, and Wayne Williams, to name a few. But if what his client was claiming was true, he was far worse.

Surely no one could have killed that many people. That would indeed put him in a class by himself and his name would be associated with it. He secretly hoped Killa wasn't pulling his leg, praying he was indeed a killer.

"So how are you today?" the doctor asked as Killa was escorted into the office.

"Cool, can't complain," he replied evenly. "How you?"

"Good, are you ready to get started?" he asked as he began the recording.

"As ever, Doc."

"I'm curious, um… Killa, how did you end up actually being a killer? What pushed you to this?" the doctor asked.

"Pushed me?" Killa chuckled. "Ain't shit push me. I wanted to be a killer since I was like eight."

Killa

"Wanted to be killer? How does one actually aspire to want to commit murders?" the doctor asked with a frown.

"A movie!" Killa announced. "A movie about a hitman. Son was super cool, dope crib, loot, plus he was murking niggas all kinds of different ways. Shit was crazy."

The meters were in the red and a bright happy face was displayed as Killa spoke.

"Yo, I never wanted to be no fireman, or rapper, or not shit like that. I wanted to be a hitman," Killa said jovially.

"So how did this manifest itself?" the doctor inquired. "When did you act on this aspiration?"

"Oh right away," Killa exclaimed. "I think I killed my first person that next day, well second actually, you know my moms," Killa added glumly, the meters registering remorse.

"At eight?!" the doctor exclaimed. "You became a hitman at eight years old?"

"Naw, the first couple were like practice," Killa corrected. "I ain't start getting paid 'til I was about fourteen."

"Practice? How do you practice killing someone?" the doctor asked.

"I wasn't practicing killing, I was killing. I had to learn how to kill, but it was hitman practice."

"Please, please explain," the doctor urged.

"Aight so check it," Killa began, both his face and the meter alight with glee.

"So, I watched that movie like err day. I would pretend to kill people every day. Stalking 'em, walk up shoot 'em with my finger, sneaking up behind, pretending to snipe 'em from

20

my window. Then one day I was rummaging through my grandmother's room while she was out. I found a trunk with my uncle's name on it. My uncle JR, he died before I was born. So anyway I opens it up, look at the pictures, old ass clothes and shit then boom there it was."

"What?" the doctor exclaimed totally captivated.

"Yo, it was a little .22 and two boxes of bullets. I scooped that shit up and closed the trunk up. I knew how to load the clip from seeing it so much. It took a second but I got it. Then it was up to the roof for target practice."

"The roof," the doctor asked incredulously. "Of your tenement building?"

"Shit yeah, nigga's been busting on the roof forever. So I'm on the way up and when I get to the top ole crack head Petey is up there smoking. This nigga right in front of the door so I try to squeeze past. Fucking junky grabbed my leg, talking 'bout gimme some money lil nigga. Talking 'bout some toll booth. I tried to pull away but dis nigga grown. Then the nigga started reaching for my pockets. I pulled out the gun and aimed at his face. I closed my eyes and pulled the trigger. When I shot dude got up and took off. I thought I missed him, but once he got about halfway down the flight of steps death caught up with his ass. Dude fell face first and slid down the steps. Blood was pouring out the hole in his forehead. I stayed there watching for a second until I heard the elevator door open then I took off down the steps and went home.

"Then what?" the doctor asked caught up in the story.

"Shit I put the gun up and laid down. Honestly, that shit freaked me out a little bit. I was having second thoughts about the whole hitman thing after that," Killa announced.

"How long did that last, the remorse?" the doctor inquired again.

"'Bout a week," Killa chuckled. "Then, I don't know, it was calling me. It was like I needed to kill somebody. It was all I could think of. I was in school picturing shooting my teacher, kids, the lunch lady. Finally, the shit got the best of me. One night G-ma was sleep so I snuck the gun out again and went hunting."

"Hunting?" the doctor asked.

"Yeah that's what I used to call it, hunting. So anyway, I snuck out the apartment and headed up to the roof. Ole Petey's blood was still there, but that's all. So I rode down on the elevator to see who was out. Wasn't too many people out so I headed over to the park on Nelson. There's, a little concrete tree house thing over there that crack heads use to smoke and turn tricks and shit. As I got close I saw a lighter and knew someone was in there. I crept up and saw it was some base head, and wouldn't you know it, motherfucker asked me for some money. So, I'm like okay hold on and went into my pocket. You should have seen dude's face when I came out. He tried to say something but I pulled the trigger before he got it out. I always wondered what he wanted to say. Son had a weird look on his face, like he was disappointed."

"Probably didn't want to die," the doctor said mortified by the story and that his program said he was telling the truth.

Over the course of two weeks Killa gave vivid accounts of murdering twelve more people in cold blood. He took breaks in between killings, sometimes months at a time, but as he put it "you can't just turn that shit off, you have to kill," Age Fourteen, that's when he started getting paid.

Chapter 4

Dr. Hill studied the results of Killa's IQ test dubiously. According to his score he had an IQ of 162 well above genius level. "How does one with this much potential turn out so... so... so... fucked up?" he wondered aloud.

A knock on the door alerted the doctor of the arrival of the person he was now most intrigued with. In short, Killa fascinated him. The man could have been anything.

"Right on time," Dr. Hill said jovially as he opened the office door and stepped aside allowing the deputy to escort the prisoner in.

"Sup, Doc?" Killa smiled obviously happy about seeing the doctor again.

"Chillin," the doctor replied as the new deputy looked on curiously at the exchange.

"Where do I sit doctor?" the officer inquired as he scanned the office.

"Outside," the doctor answered curtly.

"Oh, I can't leave this one, Doc. He's a real nut case," the deputy replied.

"You can and you will," Dr. Hill snapped. "Ever heard of doctor/patient privilege?"

The officer, at 6'2" and a solid two-hundred and fifty-pounds, was hired for his brawn, not brain, answered that he hadn't.

"Well, use your radio, confirm that you are to be out of earshot, and then get out," the doctor demanded impatiently. Killa was thoroughly amused at seeing Robocop getting chumped off. A quick radio call to dispatch sent the burly guard into the hallway. He stood at full attention at the entrance of the office while people stared curiously.

"Piece of work, that one," the doctor said setting his equipment.

"Piece of shit more like it," Killa replied. "That fuck nigga manhandle me one more time I'ma send them wolves at him."

"I must inform you that our privileged conversations do not include information of future crimes," the doctor warned.

"That was a conditional statement," Killa said calmly. "If he, then I."

"Let's begin," the doctor said starting the recording.

"So how many more practices were there before you actually became a hitman?" He asked.

"Let's see, um … I told you about dude getting some head when I hit him?" Killer asked.

"Yes, I believe that's where we left off," Dr. Hill said stoically. So far that one troubled him the most. He recalled how Killa laughed so much as he recounted the murder.

According to Killa he watched a car pull over and his friend Rico's mother jumped in. Sandra was a known junky and prostitute. Killa waited until he saw Sandra's head drop into the man's lap. He ensured the parking lot was deserted before creeping up on the car. Killa laughed as he let the man begin to climax then he put a bullet in his ear. "I'm cumming,

I'm cumming, you're gone!" Killa laughed, thinking … Dome called while getting dome.

"Doc!" Killa said a little louder the third time snapping the doctor into the present. "You done zoned out on me!"

"My bad," the doctor said slightly embarrassed. He was supposed to be unflappable but that shook him up a bit. Over ten murders and we just got to his fourteenth birthday.

"Aight, so you was asking about my first hit right?" Killa asked refreshing the doctor's memory.

"Uh yeah, no more practice?" Dr. Hill asked.

"Naw, my next one was a job," he replied.

"Expound."

"Okay, my nigga Lil J, I told you 'bout him, he running shit in the PJ's now. He tryna expand but right now he just in our projects. We had a community center where we could go play games and shit, sometime have parties, but the broke ass city shut it down. My nigga J, he paid the maintenance man to open it back up. Only now it's private. It's our shit now. Me and Rico had just started working for them niggas. Just lookouts. You know sit at the front of the projects with a walkie talkie. Watch for Po-Po, tell the crack heads who to see. So we doing lil nigga shit. So anyway, one day I'm up in the spot with Lil J, his brother Dre, and a nigga we called 'Get High' cause all that nigga do is get high. Now Lil J fuck wit' me hard ever since I seen him murk Tay so he keep me around. He was beefing about this nigga called Deezo and …

"A-yo this fucking guy short again," Dre announced as he recounted Deezo's money.

"How much this time?" Lil J asked shaking his head. He loved Deezo, they grew up together. That's why he put up with the shorts as long as he did. First it was fifty, then a hundred, now a thousand and more, frequently.

"Yo, I seen that nigga up on Fordham last week, son. Dude was spending mad cheddar, had that lil fine ass bitch, Meeka, wit' em," Get High said.

"Meeka?" Dre exclaimed. "Son dat bitch can suck the..."

"Shut the fuck up nigga," Lil J told his older brother. Even though Dre was two years older than him, J ran the show. Dre thought with his dick while Lil J had the mind of Machiavelli.

"This nigga hitting us for stacks, and you talking 'bout some bitch sucking dick," Lil J said frustrated.

"So how you wanna handle dis shit?" Dre asked seriously.

"I say we cut his ass off!"

"That's it?" Lil J asked his brother incredibly. "Just cut him off?

"Nigga gotta get dealt wit'," Get High said as he lit yet another blunt.

"What about you?" Lil J asked Killa. "How we handle a nigga stealing from us?"

"Me?" Killa stammered, surprised to be included in the decision making process. He was shrewd enough to know that his answer would work for or against him.

"I'm gonna kill him," Killa said matter factly. "Just give the nod."

"Nod nigga!" Lil J laughed. "Go murk that nigga. Take these clowns with you."

The next night Kill sat in the back seat of a hooptie as Get High and Dre argued about the best way to hit Deezo. They were parked across the street from the diner where Deezo and Meeka were having a late dinner.

Killa was irritated at their hair brain plans as he stroked the Tech 9 machine pistol Lil J gave him. As instructed he wore gloves, but was still supposed to leave the gun at the scene. That was a symbolic gesture that Deezo would get the chance to appreciate. He'd given the gun to Lil J, and Lil J was now giving it back.

"Look, look at that bitch," Dre said excitedly as they ate. Meeka was giving head to a French fry before she ate it.

Fed up, Killa got out the car and crosses the street.

"Fuck you doing lil nigga?" Dre called after him.

Kill waved his free hand at them, dismissing them, while the Tech was in the other.

Killa marched straight to the diner, pulling his shirt onto his face as he entered. He walked over to the couple's table and said, "Lil J said give you this." He then hit Deezo with four three short bursts from the Tech. Meeka only got one burst, the three rounds slamming into her chest. He then turned and left as calmly as he came. Once he reached the door, he realized he still had the gun. "Oops," he said before heading back to the table. "My bad, this yours," Killa told Deezo's corpse, then sat the gun in his lap.

He wouldn't have to worry about any witnesses since no one paid any attention when he came in. Once the shooting started they all ducked behind counters and under tables. Besides this was the South Bronx, ain't no telling. It's like Jay-Z said, even if a Jehovah's Witness witnessed it, he wouldn't testify.

"What the fuck is wrong with you?" Dre scolded as Killa slid back in the car. Get High looked at him in disbelief.

"You probably should drive," Killa casually suggested, "Po-Po gone be here in a minute."

Dre took his advice and pulled off. He made a couple of turns and parked. The trio got out and walked around another corner to where Dre's truck was parked.

"Telling J bout your young dumb ass," Dre scolded.

"That shit was gangsta!!" Get High said lighting a blunt. "You wild son."

"A-yo Doc, Lil J loved that shit!" Killa exclaimed fondly. "That's when everybody started calling me Killa.

"So you were paid for the hit?"

"Naw, I did it on the strength, but after that I was in. I was the go to guy. Oh yeah nigga's money stopped being short... well until Rico started selling."

Dr. Hill noted the sadness on the screen at Killa's last statement. However, time was up. "Okay, that's where we'll end for the day."

Chapter 5

The next day...

"So tell me Killa, how did you end up in the gang?" the doctor inquired as he read the file. "You were a member of Goons were you not?"

"Yeah, but that was some bullshit," Killa replied. The emotional meters sensed disdain. My whole project was Goon. Shit, most of the west side of the Bronx is Goon! Once you cross over 171st Street you in Fiend country."

We was like the Bloods with our red and they rocked nothing but blue. Since I grew up in the projects I was a Goon by default. Everything I owned was red. My grandma ain't like that gang shit but she knew a nigga couldn't rock no blue. Not around there!"

"So wearing blue would be controversial?" the doctor asked naively.

"At least," Killa chuckled. "Depends who sees you. See the older cats may come check you. Ask who you were? What set you claim? You know, investigate. Maybe a nigga was lost or some shit. Oh, but them young niggas, they shoot first! Even the mailman wear a big ass red hat when he come through."

"So was there some sort of ritual to join or were you automatically accepted?" asked the doctor enthusiastically.

"Nah, ain't nobody automatically in! Some niggas ain't built for that shit. You gotta get jumped in," Killa explained.

"Jumped in did you say?" he asked.

"Yeah like ten niggas beat your ass for like ten minutes! And you better fight back! Just try to cover up and wait it out ain't what's happening. That's bitch shit! You won't get put down. Nigga just got his ass whipped for nothing! Oh girls too!" Killa laughed lighting up the screen with elation. "We ain't on that bullshit sexing a chick in! Bitch gotta fight too! And they gotta put in work once they down!"

"So, you got jumped in by your gang buddies?" he asked.

"Me? Nah I got jumped in by Fiends! This was right before I bodied Deezo. I was like thirteen or some shit. I had my first girlfriend, Fatimah..."

"That girl sweating you!" Rico announced as he and Killa walked past the playground.

"Who is she?" Killa asked locking eyes with the girl who neglected braiding her friend's hair to stare.

"Fatimah, her grandma live in 1440," Rico replied.

Fatimah lived uptown in River Park towers. In the heat of Fiend territory. Killa was too young to understand the ramification of that.

"Sup ma?" Killa asked sounding far more confident then he actually felt.

"Sup yourself?" she smiled back. Fatimah was slightly older than Killa at fourteen and already well on her way to being well developed.

They kicked it for an hour until her mother Renee came to collect her. Renee was a known addict around the projects. Numbers were exchanged before their departure with a promise to call.

Those calls became nightly marathons. After working as a lookout all day, Killa spent all night on the phone with his first girlfriend.

Since a day and time couldn't be locked in as to when Fatimah would next be in Highbridge, Killa decided to go to River Park Towers to see her. Bad move.

He decided to buy a new outfit for the excursion and hit the shops along 161st Street. One of the stores was run by a Goon and specialized in all things red.

Killa selected a pair of red jeans, topped off with a white tee that read 'Goon' in big, bold, red letters. Red sneakers and a St. Louis fitted cap completed the ensemble. A large silver 'G' dangled from the chain on his neck.

He was still too young and naïve to process all the strange looks he received once the bus passed 171st Street otherwise known as the Border. And too busy playing his handheld game to see all the stares.

Killa made it to Fatimah's apartment without incident and went inside.

"Hey young man," Renee said inspecting the visitor, "you got some money?"

"Ma!!!" Fatimah yelled, mortified and embarrassed. "Don't be beggin' my company for money!"

"Girl, be quiet! This my house, he my company," Renee snapped back. *"Let me hold a few dollars and I'll leave you guys alone."*

Killa dug in his pocket and broke the woman off with $20. He would rather be alone anyway. Once they were alone he produced a new game system from his backpack.

"Ooh for me?" Fatimah shouted at the expensive gift.

"Yep," he smiled pleased with himself. *"My girl can have whatever she wants!"*

"Oh, so I'm yo girl now huh?" Fatimah huffed playfully.

"You tell me," Killa replied confidently.

"Yesss," she giggled shyly. *"Oooh, the ice cream truck!"* she exclaimed as the song from the truck's PA system reached them.

"You want some?" Killa asked needlessly as Fatimah was already headed to the door.

The couple practically skipped over to where the ice cream truck had parked to make sales. He bought her everything she wanted and a strawberry shortcake for himself.

"Let's go to the swings. You can push me while I eat," Fatimah said leading the way.

Killa followed and fulfilled the request. They were so caught up in each other they failed to see the mounting danger. He pushed softly on the only working swing as she alternated between her salt and vinegar chips and ice cream cone.

"So, since you my girl, lemmee get a kiss," he said stopping the swing and pulling her close.

Sa'id Salaam

"Nope!" she said playfully and turned her head. "Oh shit!"

"What? You scared?" Killa laughed at the horrified look on her face.

"No look!" she exclaimed and pointed to the sea of blue rushing towards them. "Run!!!"

Killa took off, but didn't make it too far. Not knowing his way around these projects he ran right into a dead end.

"You must wanna die!" the lead man announced closing in. Most of the Fiends were late teens or early twenties, but the fact that Killa was young didn't matter. Didn't even register. Dude had on all red in the heart of Fiend central. The violation had to be dealt with.

Killa knew he was about to die, but refused to go out without a fight. He was small but had the heart of a lion.

"A-yo I ain't mean no harm," he pleaded as he approached the speaker, who Killa assumed to be in charge. "I just came over here to tell you guys... to suck my dick!" he punctuated the slanderous remark with a punch to the man's jaw.

The punch didn't budge the man, instead set of the inevitable beating. Killa fought back valiantly until the onslaught of blows knocked him to the ground. When he went down the punches turned to kicks and stomps until he lay motionless.

Killa's shoes, pants and shirt were violently ripped from his body. Finally his 'G' chain was snatched from his neck

35

causing another deep scratch to go along with the other contusions.

An old lady who witnessed the beat down yelled out for the boys to stop. They didn't until she started calling them all out by name. She saved young Killa from being beat to death. Had she minded her business the earth's population would be lower than it is today.

"Are you okay, baby?" Fatimah cried kneeling beside him. "Baby, wake up! Wake up!"

Killa could hear her but his eyes were swollen shut. He tried respond but passed back out. When he next awoke he was at Lincoln Hospital with tubes in his arms.

"Oh Lawd! You up, baby! Praise God!" his grandmother rejoiced by his side. "How you feeling sugar?"

"Fine," he replied even though he felt like shit. He was lumped, swollen and had a concussion. It was actually the next day when he awoke.

"We was so worried about you! Your friends is downstairs," she sang in the sing song voice reserved for her grandson.

"How about Fatimah?" he asked urgently sitting upright. "Is she okay?"

"Her and Rico down there right now! That boy into everything!" she said. "I'ma go to church and pray but I'ma sneak you some fried chicken. You can't get well eating no white people food. They ain't got no seasoning!"

When she finished a lengthy prayer thanking God, Jesus, the Pope and everybody else, she left for church. As she walked out, Rico and Fatimah walked in.

Fatimah was crying and Rico had his head bowed. It was as solemn as a funeral procession.

"Fuck wrong with y'all," Killa said trying to laugh. His whole body hurt when he did, but it did the trick. His friends smiled and joined him on the bed.

"You aight?" Rico asked sincerely. "You look fucked up!"

"Thanks," Killa laughed. "I got my ass whooped!"

Fatimah took his battered hand in hers and massaged it. "I'm so sorry," she whispered.

"Sorry? Sorry for what? You ain't jump in too did you?" Killa chuckled.

"No, crazy," she laughed and punched him playfully. "I forget about them Fiends. I ain't think about it, and you had on all that red!"

"A-yo Lil J and dem said they gonna take care of that," Rico smiled.

The thought of revenge made Killa smile.

"What y'all gonna do?" Fatimah pleaded.

"I ain't doing nothing," Killa said pointing to the IV in his arm. "But stay at your grandmother's house tonight."

When his grandmother returned she produced a bag of chicken she smuggled in her purse. "Here boy eat this," she urged glancing around. "Y'all come on. Let this boy get some rest."

37

Rico gave him a pound followed by Fatimah who gave him the kiss he missed out on the day before. His grandmother frowned but said nothing.

"So then what happened?" the doctor asked urgently.

"Oh!" Killa laughed lighting up the screen with smiley faces. "Man, I watched the news that night and laughed my ass off!"

"Why? What was on it?" he said leaning in.

"A massacre! My niggas went up to River Park and lit that shit up!"

"A deadly night in the Bronx! A shooting police are now calling gang-related left three people dead and another four in local hospitals."

"Boy, you think that's funny?" a nurse who happened to be in the room scolded. "Them kids are in here fighting for their lives!"

"In where? In the hospital here?" Killa asked excitedly.

"Yes! Two are in the ICU fighting to live and one is in the next room," she said hotly.

Killa fought the urge to pull out his IV and go next door and strangle the Fiend with the cord.

"Okay, that's enough for the day. Let's pick up right there tomorrow," the doctor said turning his program off.

"That's what's up," Killa said winding down. Reliving all those memories, as fond as some may be, was trying. He was usually mentally drained by the time he was returned to the county jail.

Killa was alert every second and every step to and from the jail. He knew full well the State of Georgia intended to kill him and he didn't plan on sticking around for it.

Yeah, he'd keep coming to the sessions for the time being. People were fallible. That he could count on. First chance he got he planned to make them pay for being human.

Chapter 6

The next day...

"So, okay, where did we leave off?" Doc inquired as Killa got settled in.

"Thank you deputy," he said sternly to remind the bullheaded officer to leave. It was the same every day.

"Don't worry about him, Doc, today's his last day," Killa said ominously. The tone caused the doctor to look up from his computer.

"What happened to your eye?" he said noticing the 'shiner' he was sporting. Having dealt with so many child molesters he was used to inmates being beaten up, but by other inmates. Killa, however, was on high max. Only the guards had access to him.

"Ain't nothing, Doc. Remember you told me our doctor/patient privacy only applied to past crimes," Killa said.

"You like chicken?" Doc asked shooting a glance at the door. "I have extra. Too much for me."

Normally Killa never accepted anything from anyone, but after months of county jail cuisine he couldn't resist it. He was chained around the waist with the handcuffs attached but he still managed to contort himself enough to devour the food.

The doctor watched him as he stripped the chicken from the bones. He didn't, however, notice that all the bones didn't make it back into the box.

"Okay so, what happened when you finally got out of the hospital?" Doc asked hitting the record button.

"Shit, my grandma had me cooped up for a week," he said fondly. The machine registered the emotion as happy, but a far cry from the levels reached when he was recounting a murder. "I hated missing all that money, but my nigga Rico was there every day! That was my dude! I hate that... The machine changed colors and his mood shifted.

When Killa finally got released from his grandmother's apartment, he went straight to see Lil J.

"Killa!" J announced loudly as he and Rico entered the rec center. The city had recently closed it due to lack of funds, but Lil J and the Goons re-opened it. They had plenty of funds. They just paid the maintenance men to hand over the keys. Once they took over they hooked it up with video games, a plasma TV, and places to fuck.

Of course Lil J had an office, being the boss that he was. Most of the maintenance men were on dope anyway so the crew kept their pipes full and they kept the doors open.

Lil J was talking to his brother Dre and Get High when Killa and Rico entered.

"A-yo, y'all let me bark at my dog," Lil J ordered sending Dre and Get High towards the door. "You too Shorty!" he snapped when Rico didn't budge.

"How you feelin lil man?" he said genuinely concerned. "You healing up quick, B?"

"I'm cool, yo, just glad I hit one of them niggas in his shit before they got me," Killa remarked.

"Yeah, I heard. Check this, yo," he said reaching in a bag and producing Killa's chain and 'G' medallion.

"Oh shit! Where you get that from?" he exclaimed collecting it from his friend. Lil J gave him a "yeah right" look for reply.

"Leave it!" he ordered as Killa began to remove the dried blood from the 'G'. Killa shrugged and put the bloody chain around his neck.

"You know why them faggot Fiends jumped on you?" Lil J asked.

"Yeah them niggas thought I was a Goon cuz I had on all red," Killa replied.

"Thought!" Lil J exclaimed. "Nigga you are a Goon!"

"I thought I had to get jumped in?" Killa retorted confused.

"You did get jumped in. By the Fiends! You showed more heart than most of these niggas, even my dumb ass older brother!" Lil J frowned.

"What about Rico? Can he be down?" Killa asked eagerly.

"A-yo son, this ain't for him. He ain't got the brains or balls for this shit. That's your lil man, I know. Let him get money with you, but never put him in a position where you have to trust him," Lil J urged. "Look in his eyes. You can't trust that dude."

"Speaking of getting money," Killa laughed rubbing his palms together, *when can a nigga start eating?"*

"Right away. I'ma hit you with a pack, your own bench in front of 1480," he said enthusiastically. *"But first I need you to put in a lil work. You know Deezo?"*

"Yeah, that's your dude ain't he?" Killa asked curiously.

"He was," Lil J replied wistfully. *"Trust is everything."*

"Okay and that's when you did your first real hit?" the doctor asked.

"Yeah, but I did that as a favor. It was my pleasure," Killa responded, and the corresponding meters agreed it was indeed his pleasure.

Chapter 7

The next day...

"So, was there any retaliation as a result of the revenge shooting?" Doc asked at the next session. He asked even though he already knew the answer.

The doctor stayed up most of the night reading old news reports that confirmed Killa's claims. He was now starting to believe that he was actually speaking with one of the most prolific serial killers in history.

"Retaliation?" Killa laughed incredulously. "Nah, it wasn't no retaliation. It was a fuckin' war!"

Roland stormed out of Mercy Hospital blind with rage. He was the leader of the Fiends and his little brother had just passed away from wounds sustained in the shooting.

He jumped into his waiting Range Rover where his second in command, Black, was waiting. "Man them bitch ass, fake ass, so-called Goons done killed my lil brother!" he fumed. "We bout to bring it to they ass!"

"No doubt!" Black cosigned. "A-yo I heard it was behind some lil nigga was up there with crack head Stephanie's daughter."

"Aight that's where we start," Roland growled. "What about the shooters?"

"I heard," Black began even though he saw everything. He was present when the van rolled to a stop in front of their projects. He peeped the move before anyone and got ghost before the shooting started. "That nigga Dre, and Get High was there."

"Dre! Oh, he think he a gangsta now! Playboy wanna get his hands dirty?" Roland barked. "That's what's up! I know just how to get at niggas like that. Call Aisha!"

The word was on about Fatimah and as soon as her mother hit the block to cop her crack, heads were waiting on her.

"A-yo look who coming," 'P' said when he spotted Stephanie jumping from a trick's car.

"We bout to get that bread," Jose said greedily thinking about claiming the bounty on their heads.

"Hey y'all," Stephanie said approaching the men who were just plotting her murder. "Lemme get a nick."

"A nick?" P laughed as if it was the funniest shit he ever heard. "Bitch, that's all you get fo' sucking dick!"

"Shit, you can suck my dick twice and I'll give you a dime!" Jose said joining the laughter.

"No, he gave me ten but I gotta feed my daughter," she said in defense of her cock sucking wages.

"Tell you what. Let me and my man run a train on you and we'll give you a fat ass fifty piece!" P offered.

The thought of a fifty piece of dope far outweighed the indignity of turning a trick with two boys near the same age as her daughter. "Let's go!" she announced.

Fatimah looked briefly when the door opened then turned her attention back to her video game. Then looked up again when P and Jose filed in behind her.

"'Timah take this ten and get you something to eat, and bring me my change!" Stephanie said trying to get her child clear of the impending gang bang.

The plan was to fuck Stephanie then kill her but when P looked at Fatimah's body he decided to fuck her and kill her too.

"Hold up! You ain't gotta go, you can get down too," P said blocking the door. On cue Jose locked the dead bolt.

Stephanie did make an attempt to save her daughter, but a vicious right hand from P put her to sleep.

Fatimah bolted from the room trying to escape whatever her ex-schoolmates had planned. Jose was there to intercept and wrestled her to the ground.

She knew they intended to rape her and fought like a cornered animal. She put up a good fight until the two pummeled her into submission. Fatimah had to lay there as P stole her virginity.

"Let me see what this head like," Jose said pushing his erection towards her face. "Open up bitch!"

"Fatimah ignored the pain of 'P' inside of her in an attempt to keep Jose out of her mouth. Again she was beaten until she complied. Almost.

As soon as Jose pushed his penis past her lips, Fatimah clamped down on it! He screamed from the pain as her teeth cut into him.

No matter how hard Jose punched or how loud he screamed she would not let go. Not until her teeth met once she had bitten the tip of his dick off.

"Bitch bit my dick off!" he screamed rolling away holding his wounded dick. Meanwhile P continued to rape the young girl.

Stephanie had come to and rushed to her daughter's aid. "Get off my daughter!" she screamed pounding feebly on the humping boy.

Jose reached into his backpack with his free hand and pulled a snub nose .38. He walked over to Stephanie and aimed at her head. The round lifted her off P's back and across the room.

"The fuck!" P screamed startled by the shot. Fatimah got up and headed towards her dead mother. She only made it two steps before Jose's next shot collided with the back of her skull.

"So, they killed her?" the doctor asked stopping the narrative. "They killed your girlfriend?"

"Naw, Doc, Fatimah was a soldier for real!" Killa announced proudly. "Chick got shot in the head and lived! The bullet caught her at an angle that prevented it from entering her skull. It knocked her out and gave her a major concussion and brain contusion but she lived. When she woke up in the hospital she told them about the attack. Since she went to school with both P and Jose she was able to provide their real names. Jose was easiest to find since all area hospitals were put on alert for a rape suspect missing his dick head. When he showed up at a Newark, New Jersey emergency room he was taken into custody. The other boy P kept heading south all the way to Atlanta where he had family."

"And ultimately that's what led us here?" the doctor asked eagerly.

"Yeah, but it's a lot more shit too," Killa said. "You want me to skip up to dude?"

"No, I'm sorry, um... my bad," the doctor mused.

"Aight so err body knew that nigga Dre was a trick. Dudes like that is easy to get to. All you gotta do is send a bitch at 'em. And that's exactly what Roland did," Killa explained.

Chapter 8

When Aisha sashayed into Dre's little record shop, it was like time stopped. It didn't actually stop of course, it was just that she took your breath away when you first seen her. You would have to remind yourself to breath.

Aisha was in a word, a bad bitch. She stood 5'2" and had the proverbial 36-24-36 measurements. She had the prettiest light brown skin offset by mid-back length, straight black hair.

She was actually Indian from Guyana but she passed for black. The most amazing feature she possessed were a set of slanted eyes that changed colors with the weather. Today they were gray, matching not only the overcast sky, but the mineral gray 745 she pulled up in. Some cats alternated between looking at the car and her. Except Dre that is. All he saw was new pussy!

Get High stood to approach her but Dre practically knocked him down to get to the exotic looking beauty.

"What's good, ma! Can I help you?" Dre said throwing in his best smile. Even turned his head slightly to show off his dimples.

Aisha had to fight not to laugh at how easy he was going to make killing him. She flirted with the idea of just giving him a gun and asking him to shoot himself. Dumb ass might do it.

"Um...yeah, you work here?" she said feigning to be ghetto, when she was so far away from actually being ghetto.

Killa

"No, I don't work here, I own here!" Dre bragged. "And if I ain't got it, I'll get it."

"You got that single, 'Whose Pussy' by D-lite?" she said licking her pretty, full lips.

"Nah ma, that don't come out 'til Tuesday!" He said smoothly.

"That's what's up. I'll be back Tuesday then, if I'm on this side of town," she said turning to leave.

"Wait, wait, hold up, ma!" Dre said grabbing her hand. "Let a nigga take you out or something. Don't just run off. I don't even know yo name."

"Sosha, and yours?" Aisha said flirtatiously.

"Dre, but err body calls me Dre," he smiled again.

"Okay, Dre," she laughed, "but I got a little cake myself so I'll take you out. But I'm just like a dude."

"How so?" Dre asked with a frown.

"If I spend my dough, I'ma wanna fuck something!" Aisha said plainly.

The couple ended up in swank restaurant on the east side. Dre purposely ordered the most expensive shit on the menu. He had a twenty-two ounce steak, lobster, Dom P, the whole nine.

Aisha knew what he was doing but didn't mind. It was his after all his going away party, may as well do it up. He smiled smugly when the bill came like he did major damage. "Need some help? Let me know," he said.

"I told you I got it," she said removing eight crisp hundred dollar bills from her wallet, *"but the dick betta be good. If yo ass cum quick I'ma want a refund!"*

"Oh the dick is worth every cent," Dre bragged getting an erection at the thought of sexing the beautiful girl.

"Damn ma we can't do no better than this?" Dre exclaimed when Aisha pulled into the parking lot of a rundown motel near the airport. *"I can spring for a room!"*

"Nigga we just here to fuck!" Aisha said pulling into a spot. *"I keep a room here to handle my BI."*

Every human being has a sense of danger but Dre ignored his. He even saw the red Suburban full of men in red but dismissed the potential threat while following Aisha's perfect ass into the room. As soon as the door closed behind them Dre moved on her.

"Slow down, Papi," she said pulling away. *"Go get a shower. I don't suck no sweaty dick."*

Dre was naked in a flash and off to the shower. When the bathroom door closed Aisha pulled the front door open. On cue the Goons filed out of the SUV and into the room.

Dre showered quickly then stroked his dick to a semi erect state so he could make a good first impression. He came out of the bathroom with his dick in his hand, but everyone else in the room had guns in theirs.

"A-yo! Look at the look on the nigga's face," Roland laughed.

"Y'all doing it like that?" Dre complained like they cheated him. *"At least let me fuck the bitch first."*

"Only person got fucked today is you sugar," Aisha *laughed as she dug the roll of cash out of Dre's pocket. "You ain't gonna need this where you're going."*

Dre couldn't take his eyes off the huge holes at the end of the double barrel shotgun Black held. Roland scrolled through his phone until he found the name he was looking for.

"What's up nigga? I head you bagged a dime!" Lil J said when he took the call from his brother's phone.

"Naw, he bagged a nine!" Roland laughed leveling his nine millimeter pistol at Dre's face.

"Who the fuck is this?" Lil J demanded. "Where's Dre?"

"Right here," Roland replied before tossing the phone to its owner. As soon as Dre lifted it to his mouth, Black cut him almost in half with the shotgun.

The blast lifted him up and dropped him in the closet. He was good and dead already but Roland and company still emptied their guns in his face and head for the hell of it. Finally Black aimed the shotgun at his face and took it completely off.

"You know the fastest way for news and information to spread? There's three," Killa asked the doctor. Although he was an avid trivia buff he somehow guessed he couldn't guess Killa's right answer.

"No tell me," he replied as he shut down the program, ending the session.

"Telephone, telegram and tell a nigga! Only thing, a nigga gonna fuck it up," Killa said without a trace of amusement present on his handsome face. "The whole west side was about to go to war!"

The doctor scrambled to restart his recording sensing it was about to get good. He needed to record these emotions as his patient grew eerily calm.

"A-yo son! I heard that crack head Stephanie and her daughter got smoked over there in River Park," Zeke ran up and announced as Killa and Rico slung rocks from their assigned bench.

"Fuck you talking 'bout nigga!" Rico said stepping towards Zeke. "That's my man's girl and you out here gossiping like a bitch!"

"Nah son, my aunt stay up there. She told me about it. Said they dead, son. Went to the hospital in an ambulance yo!"

"Dead people don't ride in no ambulance you dumb ass!" Rico shouted as Killa looked around. He felt an overwhelming urge to shoot Zeke in his face but there were too many people around.

Instead he got up and walked to the street and hailed a cab. "Lincoln Hospital," he ordered but the car didn't move. "What the fuck yo!" he yelled. "Take me to the hospital, B."

"You got money?" the African cabbie demanded in broken English.

Again Killa fought the urge to kill someone. And as any real killer will tell you, that's not an easy task. Like Killa said before, "You can't just turn that shit off."

Somebody had to die, and soon. Killa peeled a couple twenties off the roll of drug money he had and gave one to the driver.

Once at the hospital he spotted Fatimah's grandmother pacing the waiting room.

"Um Ms. Smalls," Killa said timidly, "I'm Timah's friend." The mention of the girl's name caused the lady to break down.

"They done killed my baby!" she wailed. "My baby."

"Fatimah's dead?" he demanded roughly.

"No, Stephanie, they killed my daughter, my baby!" she sobbed desperately.

"Thank you God! Killa exclaimed unaware of how insensitive it sounded. "I mean... I'm sorry."

"Mrs. Small?" an obvious looking plainclothes cop said scanning the room.

"That's me," Fatimah's grandmother said walking over to him. Kill discreetly slid over in ear shot so he could eavesdrop.

"We should have the results of the rape kit back in a few days. One guy is in custody in Newark and we know the other one, a Paul Harris fled, but we'll find him," he said reassuringly.

"Doc, when I heard my girl got shot and raped! That's when I lost it!"

The doctor looked at his meters in disbelief. Instead of anger or sorrow, Killa was happy! He was about to do what he loved best. Kill.

Chapter 9

"Despite Lil J's best efforts he couldn't find out where his brother was. We knew he was dead but still. You know niggas be on some real foul shit leaving you somewhere dead," Killa began as the next session got underway.

"So how long did it take to locate him?" the doctor asked eagerly. He still couldn't believe his luck. This was better than any Hollywood offering. This was real.

"It was like the next afternoon when they found him. All them shots and ain't nobody call the cops, or they ain't come," Killa went on.

A crack head couple rented the room to smoke, fuck, and smoke, and found the disfigured corpse.

"We need another room. There's a dead nigga in that one!" they said not caring about nothing but getting high.

Everyone in the rec center was quietly waiting on news. Then it came. Killa watched Lil J's face as he received the news on his cell phone.

"Damn, they found him," Lil J said when he closed his phone. Everyone knew, so nobody asked if he was dead or alive.

"It was that bitch Aisha that lured him up out of there," 'Get High' announced bitterly.

"You mean that fine ass Aisha from Fordham Road?" Lil J inquired hotly. He always knew some bitch would be the death of his brother.

"I got ten stacks for the nigga who bring her to me," he said loud enough to be heard throughout the center.

"A-yo son, her lil sister work down by the stadium," Joey said. "That lil bitch fine too!"

"Bring her!" Lil J ordered before retreating into his office. Killa followed him in and lit a blunt. The two smoked until the cigar was done then sat in silence until Joey and Get High returned.

They dragged a terrified, sniffling girl in front of Lil J. At seventeenth, Aisha's sister Malaysia was already a superstar. She was a younger version of her sister only thicker where it counted most.

Aisha had a reputation for being a ruthless bitch. She was known for setting niggas up to get robbed. She got a few NBA ballers and rappers stuck up. Not to mention luring a couple to their death for the Fiends.

Her little sister was a civilian, a kid. Everyone in the room felt bad for her. Everyone except Lil J that is. He walked up to her with a snarl on his face and inspected her as she whimpered and cowered from his presence.

Without warning he savagely punched her in the center of her face. Her nose exploded sending blood flying as the pretty girl crumbled unconscious.

"Get her back up," Lil J demanded but that was much easier said than done. When they finally revived her and got her up on her feet, he knocked her out again.

They repeated the process one more time before Lil J uttered another word.

"Where does your sister live?" he asked rather politely.

Lil J and Killa sat outside Aisha's house until 2 in the morning when she finally returned. Her dead sister was bound with duct tape in the trunk of the car.

They ducked down so their prey wouldn't see them staking out her house. They were relieved to see her pull up in the BMW alone. She was so busy juggling her numerous purchases and house keys that she failed to notice the approaching danger.

"Don't say one fucking word," Lil J said through clenched teeth pushing in her place behind her. She gasped from the shock of the guns in her face but then quickly regained her composure. Black hearted bitch had ice water running through her veins.

"And how can I be of assistance to you fine gentlemen?" she said with a smile. Almost seductively. "I assume you guys are here for money and jewelry?"

She reached in her purse and produced a few thousand dollars. "Here you go fellas, hit a club. Enjoy yourself."

"You don't know who I am do you?" Lil J asked a she removed his hat.

Her face changed into a mask of fear once she noticed the strong family resemblance he shared with his brother. They were both the spitting image of their murdered father.

"You know Roland 'made' me do that," she stammered. "They told me they were only gonna scare him. They wasn't 'posed to hurt him."

Lil J just sat there quietly which only fueled her fears.

"Look, Roland keeps money here! I have his safe. A hundred grand!" she pleaded. Still J didn't say a word. Didn't blink.

"Tell him I'll give him all the money," she said turning to Killa for her appeal. "Come on lil man, tell him I'll give him the money. Wanna fuck me? I'll suck your dick! Please!"

Killa was moved by the offer and looked to his boss.

"You wanna fuck her?" he asked. "Bitch is bad."

"Hell yeah!" Killa exclaimed. He jumped up and went over to the sofa Aisha was on. She was so relieved to see a way out, she just pulled her designer dress up and slid her expensive panties to the side.

Killa pushed inside the first piece of pussy he ever had and began stroking. As he did Aisha appealed for her life.

"Mmm you like this? It's your pussy. You know that right? You can get it whenever you want it," she whispered in his ear. "Tell ya man not to hurt me. You can come fuck me whenever you want."

Killa busted a nut inside of her and got up. Not before wiping his dick off on the two thousand dollar dress. "Tell him not to kill me," she pleaded, urgently pulling his shirt.

"What it hit like?" Lil J asked when Killa rejoined him.

"Best I ever had!" he admitted without admitting it was the only sex he ever had.

"Don't ask him. Come see for yourself," Aisha purred seductively. She had long lived off her sexuality and had no doubt it would get her through this.

"It wouldn't matter how good that pussy is, it won't save you. You lured my brother to slaughter!" Lil J said getting heated. "He ain't have no face yo!"

"Please! That was Roland! They tricked me," she pleaded as Lil J raised his gun again. "I got over a hundred grand of that nigga money! In the safe. Go look."

A nod from Lil J set Killa in motion. He found the unlocked safe and the stacks of money. He dumped the contents of a nearby tote bag on the closet floor and replaced it with the cash.

He went around the lavish room raking anything of value into the bag. A wad of cash on the dresser caught his attention. It wasn't so much the money, as much as what was holding it.

"A-yo son look," Killa announced holding up his find.

Both Aisha and Lil J looked at Dre's money clip and reacted. Aisha's reaction was to run. She knew there was no explaining that and took flight.

Lil J reacted too. He stood and shot her in the back as she tried to flee. He then walked up to the squirming girl and shot her in the back of the head. Repeatedly.

"Go get that bitch out the trunk!" he ordered as he searched the house. A few minutes later Killa struggled to drag Malaysia's corpse in.

"Put that bitch by her sister and get the cans," Lil J ordered sending his protégé back out the door. Killa returned a minute later with a five gallon gas can.

Lil J poured half the contents on the dead girls then around the room. He made a trail to the door as he and Killa made their escape. A match over the shoulder by Killa set the house ablaze. Killa watched he flames in the car's mirror as they drove off.

"A-yo you ain't getting soft on me is you?" Lil J demanded.

"Never that!" Killa spat. "I'm saying though, that bitch had some good ass pussy!"

"Wow!" the doctor exclaimed as the narrative ended. "You guys killed both of the girls?"

"Well, I shot Malaysia once we put her in the trunk, but J killed Aisha," Killa responded. "I mean she did have some good pussy, but I had a girl —for a while anyway."

"Save that for tomorrow," the doctor said looking at his watch. "That was great for the day."

After the deputy escorted Killa out, the doctor sat and pondered about the young man. He actually lost count of the bodies and reviewed his notes.

"No fucking way," he chuckled astounded at the total. "No fucking way."

Chapter 10

"So Killa," the doctor began, "tell me about your girlfriend. How did she fare after the rape?"

"Not good, yo," Killa began lighting the computer screen with sadness. "When Fatimah left the hospital she came to our projects to live with her grandma. She couldn't go back uptown anyway cuz of the war."

"So how was her demeanor? Were things the same?" the doctor asked getting comfortable. He had developed the habit of reclining with his eyes closed so he could imagine Killa's stories in his mind. In full vivid color.

"Nah, not for a while," Killa replied. "She was fucked up for a minute. I had to kill somebody to make her feel better. Once I did that things was cool again."

"Please explain?" the doctor pleaded eagerly.

"Well..."

Fatimah withdrew into her bedroom at her grandmother's apartment and very rarely left. The constant gunfire in the neighborhood only fueled her fears.

Killa called and came by often but never got past the threshold. "Just give her some time," Ms. Smalls advised sympathetically.

She wasn't exactly thrilled about her granddaughter's choice in a boyfriend. She lived in the projects, she heard the rumors. She knew why everyone called him Killa. Still, it was better than watching the young girl slip deeper into depression.

Fatimah and Killa shared the same birth date and when it rolled around she was still in seclusion. The original plan was to lose their virginity together but that was no longer an option.

A rapist claimed her cherry while Killa gave his to a dead woman.

"Come on, B! Let's go do it up son!" Rico urged. "I got us some freaks from Harlem. You know them Harlem bitches fuck!"

"Lemme see what J talkin' 'bout yo," Killa responded hoping for a way out.

He had been summoned to see the man and secretly hoped somebody needed killing. "Happy birthday!" one of the crew announced as Killa entered the rec center.

"Say word, it's ya b'day lil nigga?" Lil J asked jovially. "Here nigga! Go have some fun. We'll talk about that business later." He handed Killa a stack of twenties that weighed a pound.

He and Rico hit Fordham Road to shop for the big night. A lot of dudes in the projects didn't make fifteen so it was a cause of celebration.

Killa was prepared to pay for Rico's clothes too, but to his surprise Rico had plenty of money. He had recently talked Lil J into giving his friend his own package but still, that was a lot of money. He decided to ask later. It was time to shop. The two men bought red outfits from head to toe. Sneakers, socks, T's, boxers, jeans, and hats. All Red. They then headed back over the Highbridge to await their dates.

Killa had mixed emotions about stepping out on Fatimah until he saw Thandi and Sherry step out of a taxi.

The girls could have passed for twins with their matching outfits and similar builds. Both of them were short and thick beyond their sixteen years. All the Goons out made moves on them until they saw them with Killa. Fatimah saw too, from her bedroom window.

Fatimah had only recently begun to look out the window and this is what she had to see—her boyfriend getting in a cab with some bitches.

Rico had met Sherry a few weeks ago while visiting an aunt on Amsterdam. They'd hit it off and made plans that included their respective best friends. Thandi and Killa hit it off as well and were holding hands by the time they hit 161st Street.

The two couples hit Times Square and took in all the sights like tourists. They hit the famous Bubba Gump Seafood and ate an expensive dinner.

Next stop was the movie theater but no one got to actually enjoy the movie. Rico and Sherry began making out as soon as the lights dimmed. Killa and Thandi were right behind them. When Killa's finger slid past Thandi's wet panties and inside of her it was time to go.

The youngsters tried in vain to rent a hotel room but kept getting turned away. Not only were they too young, but no one had a lick of ID. Their rolls of cash meant nothing to the desk clerks. It did, however, catch the eye of one of the bell hops.

"A-yo son," the grown man dressed in a blue suit and bell hop hat said. "I can get y'all a room," he whispered.

They followed him up a back staircase and into a vacant room. "A-yo this my spot. Ain't nobody gonna fuck wit y'all. Just break me off," he said greedily.

Both Killa and Rico pulled out their knots and the man was practically drooling. Rico missed it but Killa took note of the lust in his eyes. They split up and went into the separate rooms of the suite and got to what they were there for.

Thandi was only a year older than Killa but was decades more sexually experienced. She put him through every known sexual position. He was hitting her from the back when he heard the front door creak open. As much as he hated to pull out of her wet insides, he felt danger.

"What?" Thandi pleaded as Killa snatched himself out of her. "Shhh! he whispered as he grabbed his pistol from his pants. He didn't have time to dress so he creeped forward wearing nothing but a .40 caliber.

The bell hop was a vet and sensed that Rico was the easier lick, not to mention his knot was bigger. That's where Killa found him. That's where Killa killed him.

When Killa crept up behind him, he had Rico and Sherry at gunpoint. He already looted Rico's pockets but was forcing Sherry to blow Rico while he watched. His perversion cost him his life.

"That's right, lil mama, suck that dick," he urged as Sherry complied with tears streaming down her face. She just sucked it cheerfully a few minutes ago, but it's different with a gun pointed at you.

"Psst!" Killa whispered to get the man's attention. When he turned Killa shot him in his face. The gun was loud enough but then Sherry began screaming at the top of her lungs way louder than the blast.

Instinctively Killa aimed the gun at her but Rico clamped a hand over her mouth, saving her life. Killa took the money from the dead man before leaving the room. The couples grabbed their clothes and hit the staircase.

They ran down a flight half naked before they stopped to get fully dressed. They descended the rest of the steps and exited the hotel.

The cab driver was initially reluctant to drive the kids all the way uptown. Killa pulled out Rico's money and peeled a hundred dollars off to get the car moving.

"Good looking out, my nigga!" Killa exclaimed at the sight of the distinct pink rubber band Rico used to hold his cash. Killa wanted an opportunity to count it but gave it back. There was no need to count it anyway. It was too much money. Something wasn't right.

"That shit was crazy, yo!" Rico laughed. "I'm glad you murked that nigga!"

"For real though," Sherry cosigned. "Nasty bastard!"

"Don't worry we ain't gone say nothing," Thandi *reassured as if she had been reading his thoughts.* *"Nigga's get wet all the time round our way."*

"Word up," Sherry *chimed in.* *"'Memba last week, Hank killed Smiley?"*

"Smiley killed his brother first though," Thandi *corrected.*

"Oh yeah, that's right Meka was out there," she said.

Killa *listened to them gossip about murders the whole way uptown. He fought the urge to ensure he wouldn't be gossiped about next.*

"So what happened? Did they tell? Did you kill them?" the doctor jumped in lighting up the computer program with his own elation. He took note that he was actually enjoying hearing tales of murder and mayhem.

"Time doc," Killa chuckled and nodded towards the clock. "Gotta wait 'til Monday to hear the rest."

The doctor shut down the program and saved the session to yet another disk. The disks were starting to stack up as the court ordered evaluation dragged on. Again he wondered if the young man was pulling his leg. Yeah the stories matched up to new archives and police files, but...

To be sure, Doc called his wife on speaker phone when his patient left. He and his wife's presets were up when she answered.

"Hey dear, just called to inform you that I love you," he said.

"Thanks dear, and I love you," his wife replied dryly. The machine worked fine. They were both lying.

Chapter 11

Killa spent the long, lonely weekend working on his plan. They held him on the top floor of the jail in solitary so he had no distractions.

He was initially held in a regular dorm with other killers awaiting trial. He had a bunkmate and everything, until he killed him. They made the mistake of putting Killa in a cell with a young loudmouth who was foolish enough to rob a liquor store and kill the clerk on camera.

When the news report showed his picture that night, his mother called the police. She was so eager to have him out of her house she didn't care if it meant prison. He stole everything that wasn't nailed down. Matter fact, he even stole a few things that were nailed down. After her washer and dryer walked up out of there she was done.

The youngster made the fatal mistake of stealing Killa's last candy bar. He was already suspicious at how soon his weekly commissary was running out. Killa finally reduced himself to counting and notating his food.

Sure enough it was coming up way short. He vowed to himself that if the boy stole one more thing, he'd kill him. He did, so he did.

That got him another murder charge and the death penalty put on the table for the first charges. The town had a few murders but Killa surpassed their monthly tally in one night.

"Okay, we left off at the hotel killing. Remember you talked about the girls and you weren't sure if you could trust them?" The doctor gushed. He had waited all weekend to get the rest of the story.

"Aight, Doc," Killa laughed. He was growing fond of the doctor. He was pretty much the only human contact he had outside of the guards. "So, next morning my grandma woke me up talking about someone on the phone.

"I see you got a new girlfriend," Fatimah barked in response to Killa's hello.

"Fatimah?" he asked, now fully awake and sitting upright.

"Oh, what now you don't know my voice?" she demanded.

"Shit, I ain't heard it in some months," he replied sharply before catching his tone. *"So what's up? How are you?"*

"Don't matter how long it's been," she shot back. *"Get yo' ass over here!"*

Killa jumped up and quickly dressed. He was halfway down the hall when he remembered what he'd forgotten and ran back to retrieve it. He put the trinket in his pocket with an extra clip. The projects was still at war.

"Hey, Ms. Smalls," Killa said cheerfully running into Fatimah's grandmother in the lobby.

"You know you in trouble, don't you?" she replied. *"That girl breathing fire."* Killa pulled out the diamond tennis bracelet and held it up.

"That should get it," Ms. Smalls laughed and headed out.

"Hey, baby!" Killa sang cheerfully when Fatimah pulled open the heavy steal project door. He tried to kiss her. She pulled away.

"Hell no! I don't know where yo damn lips been!" she said hotly.

"I don't know what you talking about. What bitches you was talking about on the phone?" Killa said, prepared to stick fast to the lie.

"Come here. Let me show you something," she said leading him to the rear.

"That's what's up!" he exclaimed when the tour led to her bedroom. She pulled open the shade and pointed out. She pointed across the courtyard to Killa's bench. He could clearly make Rico out as he slung rocks.

"You saw us?" Killa said defeated.

"Yeah, nigga, I saw y'all," Fatimah said sadly. A single tear escaped her eye to emphasize her sorrow. "So, that's your girl now?"

"No," Killa said softly as he joined her on the bed. He sat beside her and wiped the tear away. "You're my girl."

"You fuck her?" she asked in a whisper.

When Killa didn't answer she knew. "Hmph. That's what I thought," she said softly. "Will you make love to me?"

"Bet!" Killa said excitedly. "When? I mean you cool now?"

Fatimah may have been upset at Killa for sleeping with the girl but it definitely benefited her. With his newly taught skills, he showed her sex was a beautiful expression of love not the *brutality that she had experienced. They exchanged orgasms until they fell asleep in each other's arms.*

"Killa," Fatimah said nudging him. "Wake up. My grandma gonna be back soon."

"Okay," Killa replied getting up and dressed. "So we cool?"

"Yeah, we cool but," she said turning Killa to face her, "I want you to cut that girl off. I mean it. Don't see her again."

"She's dead, trust me. You'll never see her again."

Later that day Killa went to see Lil J. He was immediately ushered to J's office.

"What's good fam?" Killa said giving his boss a pound.

"Chillin, yo. Shit getting crazy. Toney got hit up last night," Lil J sighed. "He cool though. He caught one in the leg. How was the birthday celebration?"

"Shit was crazy, yo!" Killa exclaimed. "Man, I had to body some nigga at the hotel! Motherfucker tried to rob us and..."

"Man, that shit all on the news! You hit a busy ass tourist spot and did it in front of some bitches you don't even know and that bitch nigga Rico!" he fumed.

"Rico cool man we..." Killa began but got cut off.

"Cool?" Lil J exploded. "Cool you say? Count this!"

Killa did as ordered and counted the money he tossed on the table. "Fifty-three-hundred," he said plainly.

"So, what's this?"

"This off a G pack! This what ya man Rico turned in."

Killa's mind shot to all the cash Rico had lately. A G pack was a ten-thousand-dollar package of crack. Each worker was to turn in seven-thousand, and keep three.

"First the nigga was a buck or two short. Let that slide. Then a stack. Now this nigga just said fuck me. Just give me what he want me to have!" Lil J lamented. "That's your man. I put him on, on the strength of you. You straighten it!"

Killa knew what that meant and decided to kill two birds with one stone. Three actually. He rented a suburban from junky Pete.

Pete ain't check license or require insurance. If you had some rocks, you had a ride. Killa had to pay him extra for this rental.

Killa and Rico crossed over into Manhattan using the 159th Street Bridge and picked up Thandi and Sherry. They headed over to St. Nick and copped a couple of bags of purp.

They smoked a blunt of the potent weed as they joy rode blasting a D-Lite mix tape. When they crossed back over to the Bronx using the 171st Street Bridge, Rico looked curiously at Killa.

"Be easy, son, gotta make a quick stop," Killa said calmly.

The girls knew nothing of the war or the border Killa had just crossed. He pulled in front of a bodega in the heart of Fiend country. "Be right back," he said and jumped out.

As Killa crossed the street, he prayed everything was where he'd left it. It was. Under a tarp behind a large dumpster, he pulled an SKS rifle and blue hoodie. Then pulled a dirt bike out from the side.

He donned the hoodie, mounted the bike and rolled out to the street. Rico looked up just as Killa let loose with the machine gun. There were no witnesses because once the gunfire began people scattered.

The 7.62 rounds ripped into the vehicle shredding the occupants. Killa made a sweeping motion back and forth to evenly distribute the gun's fifty rounds. When the clip emptied, he rushed to the truck with his pistol raised, but one look said it wasn't needed.

On cue, Pete came out of the bodega screaming that his friends got shot as Killa rode away from the scene. Killa laughed at Pete's Oscar worthy performance.

"Man, I almost hated to kill Pete," Killa announced solemnly.

"You killed Pete!" the doctor exclaimed jumping up. "Why? Why would you kill Pete? He helped you!"

"Yeah helped me commit a triple homicide and he a crack head," Killa replied. "Shit, I may as well have drove to the precinct and told on myself!"

"Damn! Time!" the doctor said sounding disappointed.

Chapter 12

The next day as Killa was being escorted through the hospital to see the doctor, he collapsed and began having a seizure. The emergency set off a small panic as they rushed to get him stabilized.

Doctors insisted that his restraints be removed so he wouldn't hurt himself. The deputy was hesitant at first but ultimately complied.

Killa suppressed a smile as he completed a test of his plan. Once he was stable, his appointment was re-scheduled for the next day and he was returned to jail. "Mission accomplished," he congratulated his murky reflection in the jails muddy metal mirrors. That was a trial run. The next time was for keeps.

"So what happened to you?" the doctor asked urgently. "They said you had a seizure."

"Yeah, I get them from time to time," Killa lied. "No big deal."

"It is a big deal. They said you were flailing on the floor in restraints!" the doctor said hotly. "I'll make sure that doesn't happen again!"

"Thanks, Doc, ready when you are," Killa said.

"Let's begin right where we left off. Umm...you killed Pete," Doc said starting his system then leaning back to get comfortable. Again he thought how lucky he was to catch this case, and remembered how he almost declined. Almost turned down the most interesting subject of his career.

"Rico's funeral was crazy!" Killa lamented. "Everybody assumed the Fiends killed him and wanted blood. Me, I was mad at Rico for doing that dumb shit. I put him on and look what he made me do!"

Right after the funeral, several of the Goons went and shot up River Park. Luckily since the whole west side of the Bronx was on alert there were no fatalities. Only a couple of crack heads that was foolish enough to be out in a bullet storm.

Fatimah eyed Killa suspiciously during the funeral. He caught it and avoided her gaze. Rico's mother hadn't smoked since her son's murder a week ago and looked like a new person already. Sometimes death breathes life.

"I'm so sorry," Killa said embracing the frail woman. He could have passed a polygraph just then cuz he was sorry. Sorry Rico was stupid enough to steal from them. Sometimes when you bite the hand that feeds you, that hand slaps the shit out of you.

Killa and Fatimah took a cab back to the projects in silence. When they arrived he paid the driver and held the door for his girl. Instead of turning in the direction of Killa's building, Fatimah headed towards her own.

"A-yo where you going?" he demanded a little more harshly than intended. "I really don't wanna be alone right now."

"I can't tell!" she snapped back. "Just tell me one thing Killa?"

"What?" he asked approaching her.

"Did you do that?" she frowned, then frowned deeper when he nodded slightly. "Damn Killa!

The war raged on for almost a year. There were drive-byes and walk ups. The body count piled up as everyone got caught up in Roland's and Lil J's pissing contest.

At their orders, shooting happened daily and as a result no one made any money. Not just the dealers but legit businesses were out of business as well. It was just too damn dangerous to sit in a darkened movie theater.

Pizza shops, laundromats, everyone felt the pinch. Soldiers on both sides were grumbling along with their stomachs. Something had to give, and it was about to.

Although Fatimah's grandmother allowed Killa to spend the night with her, she was still a deeply religious woman. She dragged Fatimah off to church every Sunday whether she liked it or not. She had been trying to catch Killa over there and finally did.

"Y'all get cleaned up and come on," she said, sticking her head in the door but not looking. Good thing she didn't look cuz the young couple was naked on the bed.

"Come on real quick," Killa said placing Fatimah's hand on his morning erection.

"Boy, no! My grandma gonna come in," she said squeezing his hardness. "Okay, you better hurry then."

He did. Killa rolled over on top of and into her. Fatimah bit into a pillow to stifle her moans of pleasure as Killa fucked her. There was no time for tenderness. He beat it up.

"Y'all come on!" Grandma yelled from outside the door.

Killa

"I'm cumming!" Killa chuckled, then did. They quickly showered together and joined grandma.

Because of the war they went across the bridge over to Harlem where Fatimah's uncle was the pastor. It wouldn't matter where they went cuz all Killa heard was 'blah, blah, blah' and it put him to sleep.

Every time he tried to nod off Fatimah gave him an elbow to the ribs. "A-yo stop that shit," he whispered sharply.

"Nope, if I gotta stay up, you gotta stay up," she shot back.

Killa got up to go splash some water on his face in an effort to stay awake. When he left the sanctuary he saw a woman who looked so familiar that it stopped him in his tracks. She looked at him and raised her hands to her mouth.

Before she could speak the bathroom door opened and out stepped Black. Time slowed as the two recognized the danger and simultaneously reached for their guns. Both came up empty as neither brought a gun to church.

"How you wanna do this?" Killa said with an evil smirk.

"It's whatever with me," Black smiled back.

"I see you boys already know each other," the woman said stepping between them oblivious to the danger. She mistook the evil grins for cordiality. "Wow, Xavier you look just like your father. Both of you boys look just like your daddy."

"Say what!" they asked in unison.

"Xavier, Rodney," she said looking back and forth between the two, "you're brothers." She went on to tell them what they already vaguely knew.

Their father had kids from quite a few women before he died. When she pulled out a picture of the two of them playing together as children, all hostility subsided.

"Well, y'all boys get to know each other, let me get back in here and see what pastor talking about."

They had intended to kill each other only moments before but now they could only stare. They could very easily have murdered each other at the commands of their adopted brothers.

The conversation started slowly and built. Once the sermon ended the two sent their people home and continued their conversation. They eventually ended up in the Halal Restaurant eating dinner together.

"This shit gotta cease," Black sighed. "Too much bloodshed. Shit's bad for business."

"Business! What business?" Killa asked. "Shit we ain't eating either."

"This nigga Roland got niggas dying, killing, and going to the pen just cuz his brother got hit," Black spat.

"Word! Lil J on that same shit," Killa cosigned. "Just cuz they took a loss nobody can eat."

"Man it would really be better if them cats wasn't around. Feel me?" Black said.

"Yeah, I definitely feel you," Killa nodded.

Both were solidly second in command of their respective gangs so in the end, the brothers decided to reunite both Lil J and Roland with their brothers and get money. They realized that pooling their resources was a win/win. Just not for Lil J or Roland.

"That is so fucking gangsta!" the doctor exclaimed. "Oh my bad. Um...well...yeah. Please continue."

"Aight yo!" Killa laughed at the outburst. "So check it."

Fatimah watched Killa curiously as he dressed. "What you about to do? And don't tell me 'nothing'."

"Aight, I won't tell you 'nothing'," Killa remarked stoically.

He'd killed plenty thus far and never really gave it a second thought. Never lost a moment's sleep. Yet as he prepared to remove Lil J from the planet he felt some kind of way about it. Lil J put him on. Gave him money, power and respect.

"I thought you wasn't involved in the war!" Fatimah pleaded as he donned a Teflon vest.

"I'm not!" he snapped angrily. He wasn't either. In the couple of weeks since he'd met his brother they both made sure to stay out of the fray. They routinely called each other to warn where to avoid or where to lure anyone that needed to be out of the way for the impending takeover.

"Killa, please don't go," she begged as he tucked a nine millimeter pistol in his pants. He didn't reply, just headed for the door. "I'm pregnant!" she blurted out as he reached for the handle.

The statement made him pause for a second, then he continued on without looking back.

"Boy, this shit better be what you say it is," Lil J warned as he navigated down the hill towards the 159th Street Bridge.

"Shit's butta, son," Killa assured him. "And for the low." He told him about a connect he made that would sell them keys for ten grand each if they bought ten or more.

Knowing Lil J wouldn't trust anybody with two hundred grand, not even Killa, he was lured away from the protection of the projects. Killa wisely talked him into bringing Get High along to watch their backs. That would allow Killa to take them both out at the same time.

Uptown, Black convinced Roland of the same deal so the two of them set out toward Harlem with two hundred grand of their own.

The plan was simple and barring any unforeseen obstacles looking to go off without a hitch. "Right there, pull up behind that caddy," Killa directed. "Tap your lights twice."

Lil J pulled into the spot as directed and hit his high beam twice. That was the signal. As soon as Black saw it from their car across the street, he whipped out a 40 caliber and shot Roland twice in the side of the head.

At the sound of the shots Killa pulled his own gun and shot both Lil J and 'Get High' in the backs of their head.

The two brothers calmly collected the bags of money and met around the corner where a getaway car was parked. Since Killa really did have a connect for fifteen a key they went shopping for cocaine.

"Yeah, Doc, that shit worked like a charm," Killa chuckled fondly. The system displayed the same as it did when he was happy. "We spent three hundred grand on twenty-two blocks and still had a hundred stacks."

"So did you guys go into business? What did you do with the fifty um… stacks," the doctor asked.

"Well, we had to wait a minute to let shit die down and start a local drought, so we just used our money to buy niggas loyalty. You know, feed niggas and get 'em high. Stupid shit," Killa replied.

"Fuck!" the doctor exclaimed when the timer buzzed signaling the end the session. It seemed like as soon as it got good, his time was up. He thought about letting the jail and district attorney know he needed more time. "Tomorrow?" he asked eagerly.

"Bet, see you then," Killa replied.

He enjoyed seeing how much the doctor enjoyed hearing his stories. He felt a little remorse knowing the doctor would one day be in the middle of one of his own. The thought saddened him. A little.

Chapter 13

"Doc, we had the whole west Bronx on smash!" Killa exclaimed at the start of the next session. "Shit worked like a charm. Niggas had been starving for so long that me and my brother were heroes when they started eating again.

By the time Killa's daughter Jessica was born he was sitting on close to a million. Literally sitting on it in a safe in his house.

Him and his brother Black bought side by side brownstones in the northern part of the Bronx. They set up house with their girls and got rich. But you know the old adage 'mo' money, mo'' problems.

"This nigga Raheem in Highbridge short again!" Killa said hotly after a third recount.

"Damn! How much this time?" Black asked shaking his head. "Guess I better holla at him."

Black was the more diplomatic of the two. When a worker came up short from time to time which happens, he'd take them out to eat and talk to them. Even give them more work to let them work it off. Not Killa! He was a Killer!

"Shit, looks like he just said 'fuck us'. This shit is like half off!" Killa fumed. "What we giving niggas half off specials now?"

"Half?" Black asked astounded. "Yeah, you better handle this then."

"Okay, but I'ma do shit your way. I'ma talk to him, hold his hand. You want me to kiss the nigga in the mouth too?" he asked sarcastically.

"Hey, I don't know how y'all Highbridge niggas do it," Black laughed. He really was pleased he was able to talk his younger sibling out of always going in guns first.

Raheem was in the rec center holding court when Killa arrived. He had all the workers huddled around telling jokes. The center of attention. Just like he liked it.

"A-yo, B, let me holla at you," Killa said going into his office.

"Aight yo," Raheem said waving his hand dismissively. "I'll be there in a sec."

The crew wanted no part of the obvious slight and departed with the quickness. "See what this nigga talking about," he sighed and went in.

"What's good fam?" Killa asked nicely as he fought the urge to shoot him in the face. "You aight B? Have a seat."

"Chillin yo. Trying to get to this money. Feel me?" Raheem replied arrogantly.

"I do, I do feel you," Killa said taking note of all the jewelry the kid was wearing. "Say, you remember Rico? Ever miss that dude?"

"Son, that was my mans!" Raheem exclaimed. "I miss that nigga err day!"

"I tell you what. If our money come short one more time. And I mean one fucking penny. I'ma send you where Rico at!"

The threat worked for a couple of weeks then the money started coming up short again. This time there would be no diplomacy.

Killa made the rounds to pick up money from the crews himself to prevent Raheem from getting it and taking his off the top. However, everywhere he went Raheem had just left.

He was thirty eight hot as he searched the projects for Raheem. He doubled and tripled back to all the spots he may have been. Finally he gave up and went to his car.

"Killaaaa!" Lisa called as he reached for the door handle. Lisa was a bad lil Spanish chick he had on his list to fuck, but now was not the time.

"Not now ma!" he said pulling the door open.

"I heard you looking for Raheem. He 'posed to come get me later," she said as she approached.

"Word! When?" he demanded.

"He say about nine. Said he gonna take me to a motel and fuck me," she said proudly.

"Is that right? Well, I tell you what," Killa said as the plot came together in his head. The trap was set. Killa admired the beautiful young girl's treachery. She knew full well she was about to lure him to his death.

"You like this dick? Huh? Tell me you like this dick!" Killa demanded as he pounded young Lisa from the back. She had her face buried in the pillow with her lovely yellow ass high in the air.

"Yeah, Papi! I love it, daddy! Mmm...give it to me," she replied lustfully. He responded by fucking her harder.

"A-yo, son, this lil bitch got some good pussy! You hear that shit splashing, B?" he asked a hogtied Raheem, who was between the motel room's double beds, but the gag in his mouth kept him from responding.

"See why you wanted this good young pussy," Killa teased. "At least you get to hear the shit."

"He fucking me good too," Lisa teased wanting in on the joke.

"Come here," Killa ordered as he pulled out of Lisa and removed the condom. She quickly complied and took him in her mouth. She was making extra slurping sounds with her mouth for Raheem's benefit. Then moaned loudly when Killa came in her mouth.

Lisa leaned over and spit saliva and semen on the man's face.

"Ouch! That's fucked up!" Killa laughed. He instantly liked the young girl.

"A-yo, you wanna smoke a blunt before you go?" he asked pulling one out of his pocket. Raheem's eyes lit up as he nodded. He must have said 'fuck it', bout to die may as well get high first.

Killa lit the blunt and took a few deep drags. He pulled the gag off, enough for Raheem to take a pull

"No way around this shit, B?" he asked without a trace of fear.

"Nah, papi, you fucked up," Lisa laughed putting on his jewelry. "How I look?"

"I gave you a chance, B, and look how you played me. Played yourself really," Killa said letting him hit the blunt again. When the weed was finished Killa put the gag back in place. "Time to go. We'll holla."

"Ooh, let me do it?" Lisa pleaded, causing both men to look at her. She was still butt ass naked asking to kill a man.

"Go 'head," Killa challenged, handing her the apparatus. She pulled the plastic bag over his head and secured it around his neck with a plastic tie.

The small amount of oxygen in the bag was quickly used up and Raheem began to squirm. Soon he was flopping around the floor like a fish out of water. Soon after he was still.

"Ooh, can we do it again," Lisa cheered.

"What? Fuck?" Killa asked.

"No, kill somebody," she sang.

He was contemplating as to whether or not he was gonna have to kill her, but instead he fucked her a few more times in front of the corpse and then took her home.

"Wow! I can't wait to hear more about her, but our time is up," Doc sad sadly. "Enj-, well, have...I mean..."

"It's cool, Doc," Killa laughed. "Actually I will have an enjoyable weekend.

Killa had convinced a female guard to bring him a cell phone. She had been sending pictures playing in her pussy. She was scheduled to work his floor this weekend and promised to let him play in it himself.

Chapter 14

"So, how was our weekend, Doc?" Killa asked cheerfully as he was escorted in. He was still amped about the sexual encounters he'd had. Officer Milton gave him a couple of blow jobs through the feeding flap on the door.

"Pretty good. You're in a good mood," he replied. Killa definitely was. Killa felt good, after two years in custody and finally getting some female affection.

The doctor noticed the screen was lit up with elation, then suddenly turned red. Dark red along with Killa's tone.

"This where it gets ugly, Doc," he said, settling in to begin. "I was out fucking that bitch Lisa when I got the call..."

"Where the fuck you been? I been calling yo ass for hours!" Fatimah yelled when he finally answered his cell phone.

"Chill, ma, fuck you yelling about? Who got shot?" Killa asked subdued by weed and sex.

"Black got shot nigga that's who!" she yelled. *"They at Lincoln Hospital."*

Killa dropped Lisa back at the projects and raced over to Third Avenue.

"Killa!" Black's girl Rita yelled when he stormed into the emergency room door.

"They shot him, they shot him," she cried as she embraced him.

"Who? What happened? How's my brother?" he said, rattling off question after question.

"I don't know who they were, they were waiting on us," she whined.

Something in her tone was off, but Killa couldn't figure out what. "They made him open the safe and they took the drugs."

Killa frowned at this, knowing no one, absolutely no one knew where they lived. They kept identical safes, one with dope, the other with cash, but no one outside of their women knew this.

"Killa, they shot him in his head!" she said before collapsing on him. As he held her his phone rang again. He saw his house number and took the call.

"Hey ma, I just got here and..."

"Ay mon, you get me note?" A heavily accented man asked.

"What? Who is this? I ain't got time to play," he barked. Killa was about to hang up but remembered the call came from his house.

"Give me da numba for da safe and me won't 'urt you family," he demanded.

"Chill, B, I'm on my way!" he said. Foolishly thinking he could save his money and his family. He left seconds before a doctor came out looking for next of kin. Black had passed away.

He called repeatedly as he sped up the parkway towards his house. He never got an answer. When he pulled up he rushed inside gun first. The house was empty except for a large amount of blood in the bedroom. Right in front of the safe.

The built in safe couldn't be moved but it was obvious whoever they were, they tried their best to get in it. They banged it with the hammer laying in front of it and judging by all the spent shells, tried to shoot it open as well. The large puddle of blood spelled torture. But who?

Killa wondered could anyone live after losing the amount of blood that he stood in as he opened the safe. There was just short of a million dollars in it. He realized he should have given them the combo. They had his girls.

That's when he saw the note. It was taped to the dresser mirror in bloody duct tape. "Money for the gals, tonight, 174th and Jerome. No bullshit."

"You won't get to spend one dime," Killa frowned as he loaded the tote bag. After loading a layer of cash he put in a little device he'd recently purchased from the Arabs on Trinity Avenue. He filled it with the rest of the money and put the cell phone that came with the bag in his pocket. It didn't matter if his family was dead or alive, he was gonna kill the Jamaicans.

Killa grabbed his new calico and two fifty-pound drums. At nine o'clock he was on the corner of 174th and Jerome as directed. The area was deserted which suited Killa just fine.

"Whata gwan!" a dread said, pulling up alongside him. Instinctively Killa raised the gun to his face.

"Easy star!" he said raising his hands to show he was unarmed. He flashed his lights and a van parked half a block up on the other side of the street flashed back.

"Gimme da money. Take de gals deem," he said, reaching. Killa fought the urge to shoot him and rush the van. The dread's eyes lit up when he looked in and saw the cash. "Okay, be easy. We pull off, you collect yaw family.

He pulled off and stopped next to the van. Another dread jumped out and hopped in with the first one. Killa raced over and pulled the van doors open. Inside he saw his lifeless baby lying next to his dead wife.

In a rage he frantically searched for the van. Then remembered the device and the cell phone. He pulled out the phone and pressed two, then send. Three seconds later the earth rumbled from the large explosion.

He followed the sound two blocks and marveled at the destruction. The blast flipped the entire van over on its roof and blew out the surrounding windows. Debris and shredded money littered the air. The sound of approaching sirens broke Killa from his daze and he fled the scene.

Days later Killa and Rita were in a Bronx funeral home picking out caskets for the triple funeral. Rita was unusually upbeat for such a solemn task and Killa took note. He, on the other hand was consumed with murder.

He wanted to kill somebody...anybody...everybody. Word on the street said it was a Jamaican posse that kidnapped his family. The crew, run by the notorious Cow Foot, specialized in snatching members of ballers' families.

Killa was so consumed with rage, he didn't hear one word the salesman and Rita said. He was too busy plotting on killing anyone he heard with a West Indian accent. He was pulled out of his trance when he heard three of them.

"A distraught woman entered with two young men. "Dem blow up mi baby!" she wailed. "Mi Darius, mi baby." The two men held her up and tried to comfort her as she picked out the caskets of her own.

Killa knew he was the source of the casket shopping outing but he wasn't done. He hadn't even started yet. They killed his family and he was gonna kill them. All of them. He fought the urge to shoot the old woman in the back of her head.

"Time to see the Arabs," he thought as a better plan popped into his head. He gave Rita cab fare and followed the Jamaicans home.

The block was teaming with Jamaicans but no sign of the 6'5" dread called Cow Foot. Killa switched cars twice a day as he staked the block out for two days.

He was in Black's black hummer smoking a blunt when he heard a tap on the window. Instinctively he reached for the glock under his thigh. He relaxed when he saw it was the *teenaged Jamaican girl who had been sweating him over the last couple of days.*

"Whata gwan?" she inquired when Killa slid his window down. He took note of her big chest squeezing out the top of the tight shirt. He'd seen her daily, wearing as little as possible and flirting every time she passed by.

"Just chillin," Killa said flirting back, "looking for my man Darius. We 'posed to hang out." A solemn look invaded the girl's face at the mention of Darius' name.

"'Im dead ya know," she said softly. "Dem blow 'im up!"

"No!" Killa exclaimed, "that's my mans and dem! We was going to eat, and shop!" Killa produced a large roll of cash to emphasize his story.

All remorse and sorrow left the girl's face at the sight of money. "You can take me den," she said and made her way around to the passenger side without waiting for a reply.

Killa popped the automatic lock and let her in. She wasn't pretty by a long shot but her body was banging. He entertained the thought of fucking her before he killed her. One thing was certain, he was going to kill her.

He took her to a restaurant on City Island where she blabbed non-stop about her family. Most intriguing was her uncle Cow Foot. Again he wondered how the feared kidnapper got on them. How did they find out where they lived? How did they know about the safe?

"'Im 'ouse not far from 'ere ya know," Inga bragged. "Afta we eat mi a show you."

After the seafood dinner Killa followed her directions up to Westchester County. She directed him to a gated mansion with a circular drive filled with exotic cars. He couldn't help but admire the cars as he plotted revenge, but aside from the Enzo, Lambo, and Porsches, it was a plain Tahoe that caught his eye.

"Can't be!" he exclaimed unable to process what he was seeing. Even when the familiar women left the home and got in the truck he still didn't believe it.

"Can't be what?" Inga asked. "Dis mi uncle 'ouse fa true."

Killa put the truck in gear and pulled off just as the Tahoe pulled out. There was no need to follow her because he knew exactly where she was going. A backwards glance in the rearview mirror at the license plate said all that needed to be said.

'Black's girl', Rita!

Killa took Inga over to some shops on the Grand Concourse and bought her a few outfits. After that he found a quiet spot and grudge fucked her in the back of the Hummer.

"You afta come to Darius dem funeral," Inga said when they pulled back onto the block.

"I wouldn't miss it for the world," Killa smiled. "Matter fact you can ride with me."

Inga was ecstatic at the offer and thanked him profusely. Killa allowed her to kiss his face before letting her out.

Chapter 15

Give this to Darius' mom," Killa said when they pulled up near the funeral home. He handed the heavy gift-wrapped box to Inga.

"You coming in?" she said with a grunt from the weight of the 'gift'. "What's in here?"

"A bomb," Killa laughed playfully. "Yea, let me park over there. Go in. I'm right behind you."

Killa watched her well-rounded ass jiggle under the inappropriately short skirt as she walked in. He regretted not stopping somewhere to fuck her one last time.

He pulled a safe distance away and watched for Cow Foot. An hour later, still no sign of him. He prayed no one opened the gift early and saw the fifty pounds of plastic explosive and cell phone.

When a hearse began to pull around to collect the body, Killa knew he was out of time. Cow Foot would have to wait. He pressed the sent button on the cell phone that came with the package and watched as the entire building blew up.

"Fuck!" Killa giggled at the huge explosion. It was more than he expected. The blast killed sixty-eight people and sent forty more to area hospitals. He debated going to local ER rooms and shooting the survivors. Ultimately deciding against it, then shooting up their block instead.

"Jesus fuckin Christ!" the doctor exclaimed. He was shocked again when the monitor showed how happy Killa was at the memory.

"Don't use the name in vain," Killa admonished. He was religious to speak of but very respectful even for a Killer.

"Time, Doc," the deputy advised sticking his head in the door. "No! We still have…" the doctor yelled, then saw that their time had indeed run out. "Yes, yes, I'm sorry officer," he offered contritely. "Time does fly," he added, stopping short of finishing the adage.

"It's cool, Doc," Killa comforted, "we'll get it tomorrow." Officer Milton was working again tonight and had a delivery for him. Another small step in his big plan.

Chapter 16

"Aight, so I called the bitch Rita and told her I needed to holla at her and the bitch was on some ole bullshit!" Killa began.

"What, she tried to avoid you? Did she know you knew?" the doctor asked eagerly.

"Check it…"

"Mmm hmp," Rita *chuckled when Killa told her he was coming to get her.* *"'Bout time."*

"For what?" he asked curiously, not understanding her reaction in the least.

"I know," she laughed, "I always knew!"

Killa was forced to sit through a flirtatious dinner, but figured it would work to his advantage. Had he just tried to take her somewhere secluded off the back she may have become suspicious.

"So, what took you so long to get at me?" Rita asked seductively across the table. "It's been long enough don't you think? I mean they ain't coming back."

Killa could only nod, fearing that if he opened his mouth the truth would fly out.

"Let's get out of here," he suggested with a phony smile. "Check please?"

They drove uptown to Van Courtland Park and parked. Killa grabbed a blanket and baseball bat out the trunk then led her into the darkness.

"What's the bat for?" Rita inquired as they walked. "So I can beat you to death," Killa said playfully.

"Well, I already know what the blanket is for," she giggled and snuggled up close. "That's our bed for the night."

"Mmm hmp," Killa replied trying to control his rising temper.

"Fatimah told me you was a freak," Rita laughed. Killa wasn't amused. In fact the mention of his dead girlfriend, dead because of her greedy ass was too much. His original plan was to get her into the woods and take his time beating her.

He even entertained the idea of raping her first to add insult to injury, but when she said Fatimah's name, Killa pulled away and swung the bat. When it collided with the side of her head it literally knocked her brains out as the bat took a large chunk out of her forehead.

She was dead before she hit the ground, but that didn't stop him from beating her head in. He was covered in blood by the time he recovered from his deadly zone.

Back in the car Killa searched her purse and found her phone. He scanned the pictures she took of her pussy and saw they were texted. To Cow Foot. He put the number in his phone before texting some of the pictures to himself. "Shoulda raped that bitch," he regretted that as he looked at her finger inside of herself.

It affected him so much he dialed Lisa and told her to meet him. "I got my period," she complained when she took the call.

"Even better," he laughed remembering how good the head was. Lisa was as nasty as she was ruthless and Killa liked that.

He knew he could use her to help him get to this nigga Cow Foot. After a blow job he had her call but the phone went straight to his voice mail.

"I know somebody we can get!" Lisa said excitedly. She was disappointed that they couldn't reach their mark so she offered someone else in his place.

"Who?" Killa asked without much interest. *"This loudmouth nigga on Ogden, talking 'bout' 'fuck Killa' cuz he the man, and he getting all the money,"* she replied.

"Is that right?" Killa asked suddenly interested.

"Yeah, daddy, that nigga getting a little money too," Lisa went on. *"I was over there the other night and he showed me his safe. It was full."*

"Well, Doc, that's how I started my next career as a stick up kid," Killa laughed. "This is where it gets good again!"

Chapter 17

"Pizza!" Killer responded when his knock was answered. "You ordered a pizza, bitch!" Isa demanded. "You here to eat dick bitch!"

"Come on don't be like that, papi," Lisa pleaded. "I'm hungry. We gone fuck, let me eat though."

"Come on!" Isa said arrogantly as he snatched the door open. Then stepped aside so death could enter.

Killa and Lisa shared a mental smile as the plan to get inside worked.

"Let me see what you got on this shit lil man," Isa told Killa. For a response he whipped out the sawed off shotgun he concealed in the pizza bag, "nice and hot!" he said.

"Oh my God!" Lisa screamed almost causing Killa to laugh. "What do you want? Are you robbing us?"

"Fuck is that?" Isa demanded, "Do you know who the fuck I am nigga? You pull a gun on me?"

"Just give him what he wants!" Lisa pleaded.

"Both of y'all shut the fuck up!" Killa snarled. "Take me to the goddamn safe!"

"Safe? I ain't got no safe!" Isa lied. "Tell you what shorty, I got a couple G's in my pocket. Take that and buy a little gear, bag of weed or something. It's cool."

"A-yo, you 'bout to piss me off!" Killa growled. "Either you take me to the safe or you gone die with them couple G's in yo pocket!"

"No, Killa! Please don't shoot us!" Lisa said blowing their cover.

"Killa?" Isa asked confused. "Wait, Killa from the projects? Fuck," he said as he now understood how deep he was in.

"You trifling ass bitch! You set me up!" he said with his voice cracking like he wanted to cry.

"Yeah, nigga, I set you up," Lisa said taking her place by Killa's side. "At least you got you some pussy out the deal."

"The safe yo! Where's the safe," Killa demanded.

"Fuck you, nigga! Kill me and you won't get in," he laughed.

"Baby, he left it open. He was showing me his money," Lisa announced. Isa looked so disappointed when he realized she was right.

"Well, fuck both of you! You gone kill me? Kill me then!" he dared. Killa and Lisa looked at each other and shrugged.

"Okay," Killa said before letting loose with the gauge. The heavy slug almost made him turn a back flip when it slammed into his chest. The killer couple rushed into the back bedroom to empty the safe.

"That's what's up!" Killa exclaimed as he raked an easy hundred grand into the pizza bag.

"Told you!" Lisa announced proudly.

"Wait!" she said as they made their exit. She stopped and dug the 'couple Gs' out of dead Isa's pockets. Killa laughed and shook his head.

"What?" Lisa asked. *"That nigga ain't gone need it."*

"Not where he's going," Killa agreed. *"Free admission to hell."*

"Yeah, Doc, I said fuck selling dope. Too much work. Buy the coke, cook the coke, bag it, and put it on the block! Fuck all that," Killa said showing pleasure on the screen. "I let the rest of dem silly niggas do that shit. Then as soon as they get their weight up, I come rob them."

Over the next year or so Killa, with Lisa's help, terrorized the city of New York. If you were getting money in any of the five boroughs you ran the risk of getting touched.

Lisa would set 'em up and Killa would knock them down. Sometimes he'd knock them off. The body count starting to add up and his name began ringing.

It got to the point that when dealers saw him coming, they paid him not to rob them. Once Killa was headed to the bodega and when the dealers recognized him they threw their money at him and took off. He had become the boogey man in real life.

Killa's name was ringing so loud that the police finally began to hear it. They launched an all-out effort to bring him in, planning to dump all their unsolved homicides on him.

Wishing to delay the inevitable showdown with police, Killa packed his guns and moved on. Lisa convinced him during a long drawn out blow job to take her with him. Every time she got him close to climax, she'd stop sucking and plead her case. Killa finally agreed just so he could bust a nut.

They drove south a couple of hours before stopping in Philly. Lisa talked him into a luxury suite downtown. Killa much preferred to be in the hood were the action was. After a week or so of smoking weed, watching TV and fucking, he was restless. He wanted to rob someone.

They still had plenty of money from their earlier robberies. This would be for kicks, to relieve the boredom. Philadelphia, like New York, had an abundance of ballers. "Ripe for the picking," as Killa put it.

Nightclubs were generally the best place to search for prey. To hunt. All hunters need bait, so Lisa hit the local boutiques in search of something seductive to wear.

"Shit!" Killa exclaimed when Lisa came out the bathroom dressed to kill. "I may need to tap that ass before we leave."

"Uh uh Killa, what if I gotta fuck one of these niggas tonight," she complained, then knelt in front of him and offered a compromise.

The couple entered the club at different times so as not to appear together. Killa first, taking a stool at the bar where he could see the whole club. The platinum and ice blinging from the VIP section made him smile. Made him hungry cuz they were looking like something to eat. He fantasized about just running up in there with a gun and laying them down.

A commotion signaled Lisa's entrance. All eyes instantly shot towards the stunning young lady. The six inch heels pushed her past the six foot mark. Her short skirt made her smooth golden legs appear to be a mile long.

The stolen jewelry she wore flashed brilliantly under the strobe light. A few clowns ran up and got dismissed by a wave of her hand. She never looked Killa's way as she posted up at a bar stool of her own. They both knew she wouldn't be there long.

"You see that bitch!" O.P. said frowning up.

"Um... hello?" the pretty brown skin girl on his lap protested. "I'm sitting right here, and you sweating bitches!"

"Shut the fuck up!" he demanded, pushing her off him as he stood. His bodyguards stood to follow him but he called them off. "Y'all chill! I'ma go bag this jawn!"

Killa saw the chump off and watched as he approached Lisa. Whatever he said worked cuz after a few minutes she accompanied him back to his VIP booth. The girl who got chumped off sulked away finally ending up on the bar stool next to Killa.

He took in the short, chubby girl with indifference. She was pretty and smelled wonderful but not his normal taste. Not until reason advised him that she too could further his cause.

Killa realized the mack wasn't an average baller, dude was rich. The diamonds around his neck were of superior grade. Over a thousand dollars' worth of champagne sat on the table. And bodyguards! Where they do that at? The man was rich!

"You alright?" Killa asked as a tear rolled down her chubby cheek. "Can I buy you a drink or some tissue or something?"

"Why not?" she replied knocking the tear away with a back hand.

"Xavier," Killa said with a smile and an extended hand.

"Monique," she smiled back shaking his hand.

"You look like you just lost your best friend," Kill said sympathetically. He'd never had the chance to become a ladies man, but his genuineness was appealing.

"I did," she replied solemnly. "A long time ago, but I just realized it tonight."

"Well, I'll be your friend," Killa said so sincerely he believed it himself. They shared drinks and got to know each other, watching O.P. and Lisa but for different reasons.

When O.P. and his entourage stood to leave, Monique sucked her teeth with disdain. "This nigga really gonna leave me? See, he 'bout to make me hate him for real!"

O.P. walked right past them without a glance. He and Lisa were arm in arm with the rest close behind. "Can I give you a ride?" Killa asked.

"If you don't mind. I stay over in Chester," Monique said on the verge of tearing up again.

Killa checked out her frame approving as she walked out ahead of him. He thought he wouldn't mind tapping that. 'May as well', he reasoned knowing full well Lisa would fuck, suck and whatever else was needed to get next to her victim. Killa didn't mind, it was part of the game.

He ran up in setups while she still had a dick in her mouth. They were partners in crime who fucked. Nothing more.

"This is it, right here," Monique *said causing him to pull over in front of a new condo building in the nearby suburb. "Um...thank you for the ride. Um...you wanna call me or I call you?"*

Killa recognized that as the 'no pussy tonight' speech and took her number. He told her he would call her in the afternoon and take her to lunch. She gave him a peck on the cheek to let him know she was digging him.

Chapter 18

Hey, papi!" Lisa sang the next afternoon when she finally made it back. *"What a waste of time!"*

"Why you say that, ma?" Killa inquired curiously.

"That nigga ain't got no cake," she said emphatically. *"Nigga just fronting."*

"You for real?" he said puzzled. According to Monique, dude had plenty of bread. She should know since they had a child together. She said he paid for the condo she lived in as well as A-6 she drove.

"Hmmp," Killa said confused. *"Well, shit, hop in and let me hit that,"* he said pulling the cover back.

"Can I give you some head instead?" she asked not waiting for a reply. What man would say no to a blow job? Especially one already in progress.

Killa looked down as he watched, wondering why she lied. The blow job meant she fucked dude. When she finished she said she had to go meet with O.P. again which only confirmed it for Killa. If dude was broke then why would she be going back?

"If she lying I'ma send her home in a box. No, in several boxes," he fumed as she showered. He took the free time and called Monique. *"Put on something cute. I'm on my way."*

"So, she lied? Why?" Doc asked excitedly.

"Time, Doc," Killa reminded, nodding towards the wall clock. "Gotta wait 'til Monday to hear the rest.

"Fuck!" he exclaimed, hating to wait the whole weekend to hear the rest of the story.

"While the doctor spent the weekend running different scenarios through his head of the unfinished story, Killa plotted. He had a court date soon and the state of Georgia wanted to kill him. He'd killed two of theirs and a lethal injection was their only get back. In truth they wanted to hang him if they could. "Ok, so check it, Doc," Killa began at the start of the next session. "I went and picked up O.P.'s baby mama that next day. With Lisa bullshitting she got bumped up from Plan B to Plan A..."

The way O.P. chumped her off humiliated her, she would be ripe for picking. So Killa decided to wine and dine her. He went to Philadelphia Customs and rented a convertible Porsche.

When he neared her condo he called her to let her know. Monique was standing outside looking like a million bucks. O.P.'s million bucks. The short skirt showcased a set of large brown thighs that almost made him drool.

In the direct sunlight of the day he also noticed just how pretty she was. "Hey handsome," she sang as she slid into the passenger seat, "I like!"

"I like too," he replied taking in her legs and breasts as they competed with the fabric of the tight skirt.

"I meant the car," she giggled and crossed her arms over her breasts.

"*I don't know what's wrong with your baby's father, but no way would I let you get away,*" *Killa said convincingly. It sounded genuine because it was. Monique was unlike any chick he'd met. Not just being a size fourteen, but class, dignity and sophistication. He was right, she was a keeper.*

Following Monique's direction they first hit Penn's Landing, where some sort of festival was going on. They walked around hand in hand and took in the sights. The couple was headed over to Dave and Busters to eat and play some games.

Killa lost to her in everything from Pac Man to pool. "*Glad you ain't a sore loser,*" *she laughed as she sank the eight ball in a side pocket.*

"*Why would I be?*" *Killa chuckled.* "*I'm letting you win.*"

"*Letting me?*" *she laughed.* "*Yeah right! I'm killing you!*"

"*Bet something then!*" *he challenged.*

"*That's what's up. You can have what you want if you beat me,*" *she offered.*

"*And what's that?*" *Killa asked.*

"*Well, since you keep staring at my ass every time I shoot...*"

"*And if you win?*" *he asked seriously.*

"*You still get some,*" *she laughed.*

"*That sounds like a win/win to me!*"

"*Wow!*" *Killa marveled at the voluptuous girl as she lay naked on her bed.*

"*I hope you wow me too,*" *Monique said seductively. He did.*

The couple spent the night making love some more. It wasn't all pleasure as Killa probed for information. When he left the next morning he knew all he needed to know, about Lisa.

She was lying. Dude had a couple hundred grand in a safe at his row house. Millions more in banks.

Knowing O.P. and Monique's daughter would be the benefactor of these millions after he killed him Killa began thinking long term.

Monique was a pre-med student set for med school in Atlanta. A couple hundred grand more to go with what he had would set him up nicely. Not to mention the million or two more from the future dead guy.

When Killa got back to the hotel the next morning he walked in on Lisa frantically searching the room. "What you looking for ma?" he asked knowingly. His eyes shot to the room safe where he once kept the money. It was empty and open. He left it empty and closed.

"Huh? Oh nothing. I mean my ring," she stammered. "Where's our money?" Lisa asked casually. "I need to go shopping."

"I'll take you later. I put the cash up," he replied not saying where 'up' was. 'Up' was a floor up where he rented another room.

"That's cool. I gotta go meet with dude again, see what this nigga talking about," Lisa said offhandedly.

"The broke guy?" Killa asked looking at the diamond necklace with 'O.P.' written in diamond on the medallion.

116

"Yeah with his frontin' ass," Lisa laughed. "You want some head before I go?"

"Nah, I'm cool," he replied. He wasn't the least bit surprised when he came back to the abandoned room the next day. It looked as if Lisa tossed the entire room upside down searching for valuables.

Killa knew it was time to move as well and went upstairs to pack. He loaded the rest of his cash in a backpack and put it over his shoulder. He placed a fully automatic MAC-11 equipped with a silencer in a tote bag so he could keep his finger on the trigger.

In the parking lot he saw four men staking out his Hummer. The Porsche was too close to get to without being seen so he said 'fuck it' and headed to the truck. The men let him get to the truck before approaching.

When they got close enough, Killa spun and fired a full clip silently from inside the bag. The first two men died instantly. The other two ducked for cover behind their van.

"Amateurs," Killa laughed as he snuck around from their flank. He slipped another thirty round clip in as they peered out looking for him.

"Psst! Right here," Killa whispered as the MAC whispered death into one of the men's ear. The other dropped his gun and raised his hand.

"We need to talk," Killa said calmly. He didn't have to ask again. The man told him Lisa give him up to O.P. and O.P. sent them to kill him. The man gave up everything he knew. He

rattled on and on in an effort to save his life. He talked so much Killa had to kill him to shut him up.

Monique confirmed a lot of the dead man's information unknowingly. Killa extracted what he could from her comparing it to what he learned. He overheard her speaking with a girlfriend complaining that he told her she was cut off.

"Girl, he done moved some Spanish bitch up in there now talking about bring him his keys, and I better not come over there cuz his girl..."

Killa immediately took her keys and had every one of them copied. It was time to make a move. Monique was set to move to Atlanta to attend medical school and begged him to come. When Monique's daughter asked him, he finally agreed.

"I got a little business to handle before we can go," he related.

Chapter 19

A-yo, Doc, they had me on some mission impossible shit!"
Killa laughed. "I staked dude out for two days straight!"

*Killa had to use what he knew and what he saw to develop
a plan. Common sense told him to abandon the plan but Lisa's
betrayal had to be addressed.*

*Lisa was born and raised in the Bronx, so she knew the
rules. Death before dishonor!*

*After several days of waiting Killa finally saw his chance
and took it. By now he knew that duffle bags meant cash. He
licked his chops when three bags came at the same time. Killa
was close enough to hear O.P. give his guards a night off.*

*"Y'all niggas fall back tonight. Hit a club or something,"
he advised. "I be wanting to fuck my bitch all over the house
but y'all niggas running around.*

*Killa watched them leave and waited. Then he waited, and
waited some more. As he waited and watched their movements
throughout the house, lights turning off and on.*

*Finally he took a deep breath and stepped out the rental
car. "No turning back now," he said cheering himself on. He
had, by the process of elimination narrowed the key down to
two. His luck was good and the first one turned the lock.*

*Sounds of vigorous sex wafted down the steps as Killa
ascended. He felt himself getting hard from Lisa's 'aye papi'
screams. "Nasty bitch!" He fumed mentally.*

"A-yo, get it from the back!" Killa chuckled as he entered the room. O.P. had an ankle in each hand fucking the daylights out of Lisa.

"I am," he replied, until his mind caught on. He spun around wide eyed, staring at the MAC with the silencer staring back. "What the fuck!"

"Bout time!" Lisa said pushing him off. "Get the fuck out of me!"

Killa had to laugh at how quickly she switched sides. "'Bout time huh? Poor thing just been waiting on daddy?"

Lisa jumped up and took her side by Killa. "The money in the next room," she said.

"Damn, son! You see what kind of snake you was in bed with?" Killa asked the still silent man.

"Just part of the game, yo. I slipped and it's gonna cost me a little bread," O.P. said diplomatically.

"It's gonna cost you a lot more than a little bread nigga!" Killa snarled. "You tried to kill me, B."

"And you killed four of my best dudes, so take the little money and bounce. Not to mention you got Monique and my daughter. Oh, what, you ain't think I knew? I spared you now spare me."

Lisa was conflicted. If Killa spared him then he would definitely cut her off. If he killed him he'd probably kill her too. She had to roll the dice.

"That nigga tried to murder you. baby! That's all he talked about! Fuck him!" she yelled pushing the gun towards O.P.

"You wanna kill him?" he asked handing her the weapon. As he did he pulled a second gun from his back. No sooner than Lisa took the gun she squeezed its hair trigger. It silently sent twelve rounds rushing at him.

"There, daddy!" she said handing the smoking gun back. "Bodied his ass for you! Come on I know where the dough and dope is," she said leading him to another room. Neat piles of money were stacked inside of two duffle bags.

"You must have got my message," Lisa said desperately. "I had to play along, daddy."

"That's what you were doing? Playing?" Killa spat angrily.

"That's right, daddy," she begged dropping to her knees. "Come on, baby, let me make it up."

Lisa opened her mouth but instead of dick she felt the hardness of the silencer. The next thing she felt was death as Killa pumped a three shot burst into her open mouth. "You guys look good together," Killa teased the body as he stepped over it.

He was halfway down the steps when the front door opened. In walked the two bodyguards with guns in hand.

"What the f-," was all the lead guard got out before barrage of quiet slugs tore into him. Killa tossed the empty machine gun to the floor and pulled the nine.

The second guard took advantage of the lull and came up firing. Killa grunted as the .45 Cal ACP rounds slammed into his chest at eight hundred feet per second. The impact against the bulletproof vest sat him on his ass on the steps.

The guard mistakenly thought he'd done some major damage and lowered his weapon to inspect the intruder. It was a mistake he would not live to regret. Killa popped up and popped the careless guard right between his surprised eyes.

He then made his exit, gun leading the way like a flashlight. With the coast clear he rushed to his getaway car and got away. A smile spread across his face even though the slugs felt like he was kicked by a horse.

"How much was in the bag?" the doctor asked. Curiously.

"Just short of half a mil," Killa replied lighting the program screen with joy.

"Fuck! What did you do with all that money!?" he asked eagerly.

"Made the worst mistake of my life," Killa said changing the screen colors to remorse. "I came to Atlanta."

Chapter 20

"*Welcome to Atlanta* the sign said," Killa chuckled humorously.

The doctor inwardly sighed knowing they were nearing the end of the narrative.

He had the official police reports, but was very interested in hearing his patient's side of the story. The doctor had worked with the state long enough to know they were liars.

"We bought a nice three bedroom condo with O.P.'s money. It was downtown in Atlantic Station," Killa began.

Monique began medical school leaving Killa with too much time and money on his hands. He wandered the streets of Atlanta aimlessly until he finally decided to do something with himself. He ran into an old friend from the Bronx who was now the rapper known as D-Lite.

The conversation resulted in Killa getting into the business of music, robbery and drugs. Killa excelled in this new endeavors as well.

Killa Sounds *specialized in all genres of music to cater to the demographics of the diverse city. He had become legitimate. A business, a taxpayer, and more importantly, a father.*

A year after moving to Atlanta, Monique had given birth to their son. He had everything to live for, but a chance encounter gave him something to kill for.

One day a loud Jamaican couple entered the store. They both had on a ton of tacky jewelry intended to show their wealth, but instead inadvertently showed their lack of class.

Both had mid length dreads and smelled of oil and weed... The woman marched up and down the aisle with the man in tow. She was pulling any and everything off the shelves and tossing it into the basket.

"Mi can't believe dem no 'ave 'til Shiloh!" she griped. "What kinda store don't 'ave Buju!"

"Ma'am, if it's Buju you want, it's Buju you'll get," Killa smiled. He had several employees but spent a great deal of time at the store none the less. "Just leave your name and number and we'll call you when it comes in.

"Cow Foot!" the woman called drawing the man near, "Give the gal dem da number."

Killa reached for his empty waist at the mention of the name of the familiar looking man. A million painful memories came flooding back culminating in the vision of Fatimah and his daughter with their throats cut.

"Just put me name 'pon di paper," Cow Foot asked Killa who fought the urge to come across the counter and attack. He was shocked that the notorious kidnapper and murderer was henpecked.

"Address too," Killa said planning to use it real soon. "Nice chain," he added complimenting the gaudy multicolored old school Gucci link.

"Me 'ad dis ting fa years ya no. Man make it for me in the Bronx. That's where me from."

"Sho nuff!" Killa said in his best southern accent. "My mama dem from up that way. Where about you stay?"

Again Killa fought the urge to murder the man on the spot when he gave the right answer. No question this is the man responsible for the death of his family.

He walked out behind the couple and took note of the custom SUV they drove off in. He thought about following them but he had a more pressing need. Killa needed a gun.

There were gun stores and pawn shops all over metro Atlanta but Killa had no intention of filling out any forms. No, he wasn't buying it for sport, or hunting or home protection. He planned to kill a man. His wife too for marrying him.

He traveled to the impoverished area of the city and purchased a stolen police .40 cal. For good measure he copped a bag of weed to remember how well a blunt goes with a body.

Always the professional, Killa stalked his victim for a month. The logistics were crazy to get in the upscale community, kill the couple and get out clean. In the end he had to weigh the cost of revenge with the possibility of getting caught.

He was now a husband and father, a business owner. He was respectable. He was a killer. He was Killa!

When the big day came, Killa was a bundle of nerves. Monique noticed and questioned him about it. Especially after he made love with her like it was the last time.

After his family left Killa donned his disguise. He put together a fake police uniform complete with badge and holster. Close inspection would prove it fake, but the only ones who would get close enough, wouldn't live long enough to tell anyone.

"Ooh knocking 'pon mi door like da police de!" the woman demanded snatching the door open. The plan changed in an instant when he saw two small children by her side.

There was no turning back now. He was amped past the point of no return.

"Whatever you want, talk wit' mi 'usband," she said pushing past Killa with the kids. She loaded the tacky kids into the truck and pulled off while Killa stood in the open doorway.

A cloud of weed smoke greeted Killa as he walked into the den. The victim was leaned back in a large recliner pulling on a huge joint.

"Mind if I smoke with you?" Killa asked as he entered the cluttered room.

"Blood clot! Ooh you?" he said preparing to jump up. When Killa pulled the weapon from his holster the man sat back down.

"Ras clot, you know ooh I am! You pull a gun 'pon mi? In mi 'ouse!" he snarled.

"Shut the fuck up!" Killa said emphasizing the command with a slap of the gun. Then the strangest thing happened. Cow Foot began to plead for his life, but minus the accent.

"A-yo, be easy man. You want money, weed? Here!" he said thrusting the huge spliff at him.

"I'm from the Bronx too," Killa said taking a toke of the weed. "You don't remember me do you? You have no idea of why you're about to die?"

"Look homie that was a long time ago. You can't hold a grudge like that, B," he pleaded.

"Hold a grudge!" Killa snapped. "Nigga you cut my daughter's throat! My girl! My brother!"

"I don't even know who you are! Who are you?" Cow Foot begged. The man was actually crying from the fear.

"I'm Killa! Can you hear me now?" Killa yelled.

"Killa!" he replied, now understanding how short his life span had been reduced. This was the man who blew up a funeral home full of mourners just to get at him. Yeah he was ruthless in his day, but a funeral home.

Cow Foot pushed himself off the recliner in an attempt to fight. There was no talking or even paying his way out of this one. He took exactly two steps before the .40 cal sent him back ten. He tumbled over the recliner landing on his face.

"Turn over!" Killa demanded, standing over him. "I want you to see it coming!"

"Naw, man chill!" Cow Foot begged. "Man I won't do that shit no more! That's my word!"

"Do what?" Killa barked. "Won't cut my girl's throat? My baby?" he punctuated the statement with a leg shot.

The wounded man yelled at the top of his lungs. He was summoning help from everything he could think of, but got none. Instead Killa shot him again, then again. Non-lethal leg

127

and arm shots to inflict as much pain as possible. As much noise as possible too.

The gunshots in the affluent area were an oddity and noticed by all. Fifteen 911 calls were placed sending half the precinct. Since Killa only had the one clip he saved the last round for the coup de gras.

"Open up, you piece of shit!" he ordered shoving the large barrel in his mouth. Killa pressed it against his tonsils and pulled the trigger taking what was left of his life out the back of his dreaded head.

Killa rushed out into a sea of blue. "Drop the gun! Raise your hands!" came the command. In an instant Killa had to decide if he wanted to live or die. Had he had one bullet left he would have tried them.

"Shit, Doc, there was about fifty white niggas with guns! Them niggas was drooling!" Killa laughed. "I ain't have no chance so I laid it down."

"They would have killed you, no question about it," the doctor offered.

"Shit, they still trying to kill my ass!" Killa shot back.

The session was over but the program was still running and registered fear. It was an emotion that had not been recorded up until this point.

"And that scares you?" Doc asked eager to explore the breakthrough, but it changed to anger in an instant.

"Don't shit scare me, Doc! I'll kill the whole state of Georgia before I let them kill me!" he snarled.

Chapter 21

"Okay," Doc began as he pressed the space bar to start the recording. "What happened at the jail? With your bunkmate?"

"Man, that nigga wouldn't shut up," Killa laughed showing amusement and frustration on the screen.

Where you from? I'm from southwest. What you in for? You got a bond?" the eager young man rattled nonstop questions as Kill entered the cell that would be his home until he went to trial.

"Some trial," Killa mused to himself. When he surrendered and the police went inside he knew it was over. He tortured Cow Foot with multiple gunshots before finally killing him. It was malice murder in the purest form.

The makeshift police uniform he wore only made it appear more sinister.

"Shit Shawty, I got a body! Kilt me a nigga the club..."

Killa tried his best to tune the man out but he would not be ignored. Not only was he a motor mouth but he was touchy. He kept touching Killa's arm to ensure he had his full attention.

"Check it homie, I got a lot on my mind," Killa said almost pleading, "so I really don't want to kick it right now. Let me get myself together. We'll talk later. Aight?"

The big mouth paused for a few seconds with a confused look on his face. "So, um... you play chess? I play chess. We can play chess! I played everybody in here. Nobody wanna play now cuz..." *he rambled on and on. The man talked even after Killa laid down and pretended to be asleep. "I got cousins in New York! You know a girl named Michelle? She got a brother named Michael? Y'all got some pretty women down there, oops up there, we 'down' here, but we got some pretty women down here too," he said without taking a breath. When he did pause for a breath it was only to launch another run-on sentence.*

"After two days I just couldn't take it anymore," Killa laughed, his pleasure evident on the screen. His mood didn't change even when he detailed strangling the man on the toilet.

"See Doc, we spend a lot of time locked in them cells. So when they let us out we take turns using the bathroom. We try not to shit while we in there together," he explained. "But you ain't always gonna make it. Now, I done told dude about talking to me while he shits! Told him three, four times! Warned him, threatened him, but would he stop? Fuck naw! Nigga farting, shitting and running his gotdamn mouth! Grunting and straining like um... sooo I-I had to kill him, Doc." Killa laughed as he detailed jumping off the top bunk and choking him to death. He left him right there on the toilet with the bed sheet around his neck.

After that the state declared their intention to seek the death penalty. That's when Killa declared his intention to escape. If it was just a matter of him doing some time so be it. It's part of the game. Anyone who gets their daily bread from the streets knows jail is a part of it. But now it was a matter of self-defense. Killa didn't mind dying while fighting to live but to sit there and wait for someone to kill you?

"Fuck I look like? A sheep or some shit!" Killa exploded, sending the screen into the deepest red yet. It was a matter of survival.

"So, what about your wife um… Monique? How did she adjust to the situation?" Doc inquired. He was sad that it was over. Killa had laid out his entire life up until the present day. This would be the last session.

"She left! Dirty bitch dropped the kids off back in Philly and I ain't heard from her since!" Killa said showing anger. "I… I… argh!" Killa was cut short by a grand mal seizure.

"Help! Help! I need help!" the doctor screamed as he ran out into the hall. The deputy was the first to respond. Remembering the ass chewing he got about the restraint last time he scrambled to unshackle the convulsing man.

"Easy, buddy," he said undoing the handcuffs and waist chain. The second the last ankle chain came off Killa sprang into action. He plunged the sharpened chicken bone into his jugular vein.

Blood shot to the ceiling as the near dead officer plunged to the floor. Killa jumped up and pulled off the bloody jail uniform revealing a short set underneath. He then pulled the dead deputy's gun and turned towards the door. He and the Doc shared a dangerous silence as he re-entered the room. Killa meant what he said about killing the whole state of Georgia before he let them kill him.

But Doc? He really didn't want to kill the doctor.

"Here!" the doctor said extending his car keys and saving his life in the process. Killa looked at the keys, the gun, and then the doctor.

"It's the blue Honda, hit the alarm and it will chirp," he said eagerly. He held back from asking to go with him. After what seemed like minutes Killa took the keys and rushed from the office.

He hit the stairway and descended each flight in two leaps until he hit the ground floor. He tossed the doctor car keys aside once he spotted his own ride. A smile spread across his face as he made his way to the car.

"Fuck so funny?" Monique snapped as he slid in the passenger seat.

"Just happy to see you!" Killa exclaimed as they pulled off.

"Well, I'm happy to see you too. Now let's get the hell out of this backward ass state!"

"Not so fast! I have some unfinished business before we can leave," Killa fumed. "No one knows you're down. You have a chance to go back to your life."

"You are my life! The kids are with my mom. I told you ride or die, don't make me a liar!" she said adamantly. Killa fought the urge to dismiss her and send her back, but didn't.

"Ride or die then!" he laughed as they made their way to the hideaway.

After a year in custody Killa spent the next month inside of Monique. In between bouts of sex, they watched news reports about them. Of course Monique was the first person they turned to, to search for the escaped killer. Once it was discovered that she dropped out of school and abandoned her life she became a suspect.

"No they didn't!" Monique fumed as her picture flashed on the screen. "They know they coulda put a better picture than that up there! Got me looking all crazy!"

"You on *America's Most Wanted*, and you complaining about your hair," Killa laughed. The situation was far from amusing. With her now a suspect they lost access to the money she had in her accounts.

"What we gonna do about old girl?" Monique asked knowing Officer Milton was on her way expecting to be paid for her help in the getaway. "We can't get to our money."

"Handle it!" Killa said handing her a pistol. "See if she can wait. If not…"

"Fuck y'all mean I can't get my money?" the crooked officer demanded when Killa explained the situation. "Nigga, I been looking out for you while you was in there. Feeding you, sucking your damn dick, and got your ass a phone!"

"Sucking his dick!" Monique demanded. "What she mean by that? Bitch, I wasn't paying you to fuck my man, just look out for him."

"Well, I threw that in for free!" she spat back. "Now, y'all got a reward on y'all head three times what y'all owe me so um…" The officer didn't quite get to finish the threat before Monique shot her.

The force of the bullet knocked her down but did not penetrate the bulletproof vest she wore. She pulled her own weapon and began shooting back. Killa scrambled to get his gun from the next room while the women engaged in a close range gun battle.

Monique who had never fired a weapon before that day didn't stand a chance. Officer Milton was as crooked as they came but none the less she was the police. The weapons training and range time paid off and she came out on top. Two well placed upper torso shots killed Monique instantly.

The first thing Killa saw when he returned with a gun was Monique's dead eyes. Then a volley of shots rushed towards him. Killa dove for cover to escape the barrage.

"'Bout empty ain't cha?" Killa asked hopefully.

"Come see, muthafucka," the officer spat, "stick ya head out!"

Since they had chosen to hide out in plain sight it was a matter of minutes before the place would be crawling with police. There would be no peaceful surrender this time. Not with the beloved deputy he killed family on the news every night.

"Ride or die," Monique's voice echoed in his head.

"Ride! Cuz dying ain't an option!" he replied and came up shooting. Killa leaped over the sofa where the cop was and took a round in his shoulder mid-flight. Still he landed in front of the woman and finished her with a head shot.

Killa grabbed a shirt to hold the wound and took off out of the apartment. Besides the pistol he was empty handed. The first of many units responding to the call of shots fired pulled up just as Killa pulled off. Had the officer not been so intent on checking the address he would have looked Killa straight in the face. And would have died for it. He was a wounded animal. Nothing is more dangerous!

Chapter 22

"Oh!" the doctor's wife gasped upon entering their home and seeing the bloody stranger. The doctor stifled a smile, oddly happy about seeing his patient alive.

"How badly are you hurt?" he asked approaching.

"Is this... Is this your patient? The one on the news?" his wife demanded. She was confused by the show of concern. "I'm calling the police!"

The doctor practically tackled her to prevent her from reaching the phone. "No!" he yelled. "He won't hurt us. Let's just do what he says!"

Killa couldn't hurt them right then if he wanted to. His brain ordered his arm to lift the gun and shoot the woman but got no response. "I'm fucked up, Doc," he said barely above a whisper. He'd lost so much blood only immediate medical care could save him now.

"You'll be okay," the doc said looking at the wound. "Went right through. I'll stop the bleeding and you'll be fine."

Killa closed his eyes and drifted off. The last thing he heard was he doctor's wife again announce she was calling the police.

When he awoke those last words were the first words he remembered. Killa expected to feel the unforgettable feel of cuffs and shackles when he awoke but didn't. Instead he awoke in the couple's plush poster bed in the master bedroom.

The doctor's wife was hogtied and gagged on the floor beside the bed. "What the fuck?" he mumbled.

"Look whose up!" Doc exclaimed coming into his blurry view.

"Oh her?" the doctor chuckled. "Kept trying to call the police. Not to mention she had to donate a few pints of her universal blood. See honey, you finally became of use to me!" His wife squirmed and cursed him through the gag.

"You trippin son!" Killa laughed sitting up. "What you gonna do with her once I leave? She's definitely gonna call the police on you."

"Kill her for me. Please? Before you leave kill her," the doctor pleaded. "I got the story all worked out. You burst in, held us captive, made me fix your shoulder. Than strangled the miserable life out of this miserable bitch! Please! Please kill her?"

"Kill her yourself! Try it. It's fun," Killa chuckled at the doctor's remarks. "It'll make you feel better."

"You think?" the doctor asked eagerly.

"I don't think, I know! Trust me, you'll love it!"

That's all it took for the doctor to pull his belt and put it around his wife's neck. He screamed as he choked the struggling woman. Even bound head to toe she put up a good fight. It took the out of shape doctor several minutes to end her life. In the end he sat there huffing and puffing in an attempt to catch his breath.

"Killa," he began sheepishly, "My dick is rock hard! It is supposed to do that?"

"Happens sometimes," Killa laughed. "Thought you was gonna bust a nut the way you were howling."

"God that felt good!" the doctor exclaimed. "I wish her bitter black hearted mother was here too! I'd love to choke that old bag!"

"Wait at least a couple hours before you call the police," Killa advised as he put the finishing touches on the doctor's knots. The plan was to leave him tied up near his wife and blame everything on the already wanted man. He gave him all the available cash and an ATM card and code.

He would only be able to take out the fifteen hundred dollar daily limit before the card would be reported and traced. It didn't matter cuz Killa didn't plan on going too far. He like Atlanta and had no plans on leaving. He knew the first place they expected him to go would be New York so he stayed put. Instead of running, Killa hid in the seedy motels along Fulton Industrial Boulevard.

Killa laid low for weeks watching himself on the news. He only slipped out at night to buy weed or money orders to pay for the hotel room.

The local whores offered the handsome young man their wares at discounts or free, by he always declined. It wasn't that he didn't want a woman he just didn't want AIDS.

"Hey, baby," a reluctant and exceptionally cute young woman called out as he returned to his room. Killa only nodded and kept moving.

"Bitch, you betta get that nigga!" her pimp demanded from his car. "Come back without some money and I bet I beat yo ass!"

"Hey, Mista! Please," she pleaded causing Killa to stop. The last thing he needed was unnecessary drama around him.

"Come on, come on," he demanded to cut down the racket the pimp was making.

Killa had seen the flashy young man around the hotel often and knew he didn't mind beating up one of his girls. This was a new one he noticed and she was even prettier in the light.

"He said you gotta give me a hundred dollars, and um…you only got twenty minutes!" she said like she was just coming out of training.

"Well, sit over there for twenty minutes and be quiet," he said hotly. His money was running low and he hated wasting a hundred dollars for nothing.

"You don't wanna have sex with me?" she asked curiously.

"Dang!"

When she crossed her legs and exposed her red panties Killa had a change of mind. "Matter fact, let me see what it hit like!" he said. On cue the girl walked over and produced a condom. Killa put it on as she removed her panties and bent over on the bed. "Shit!" Killa exclaimed as he pushed himself inside her tight vagina. "Shit," he exclaimed again minutes later when he climaxed. "Pussy brand new!"

"Fuck, got twelve minutes to spare," he laughed.

The girl winced in pain as she pulled her panties back up. "That shit hurts!" she griped.

"Never heard a prostitute complain about dick."

"I ain't no prostitute!" she exclaimed hotly. "Flash making me do this! He gone beat my ass if I don't make him a thousand dollars."

"How much you made so far?" Killa inquired washing his dick in the sink.

"This hundred," she said putting the money in her small purse. "Only gotta fuck nine more strange men and give all the money to Flash to buy more jewelry! Boy, he making a lot of money and I ain't even ate."

"How much is a lot?" Killa asked curiously. He was already hot about the cute young girl being pimped, and wouldn't mind robbing him.

"He bought our grandmother a Cadillac last year before she died."

"Y'all grandmother?" Killa asked puzzled. "You and Flash related?"

"He my cousin," she said shamefully. "My momma kicked me out for smoking weed. I ain't have no place to go so I went over there. First thing he do is rape me, then brang me out here!"

"Say, bitch!" Flash yelled as he banged on the hotel door. "I know y'all better open this damn door!"

"I swear if I had a gun," the girl said cowering from fear.

"I do," Killa sighed. The last thing he wanted or needed was drama.

Flash started kicking the door as he yelled, "Open dis gotdamn door!"

"He gone kill us!" the young girl screamed.

"No, he's not," Killa said cocking his weapon. The door flew open and Flash ran in. "Easy homie, take ya chick and push," he warned.

"I ain't going nowhere with him!" she yelled coming behind Killa.

"Renee, I know you betta brang yo ass on!" Flash said approaching. "And stay out my business, nigga." Killa could only shake his head at what he knew was coming.

Flash reached in his waist and grabbed his gun. Killa whipped his own out from behind his back and fired. When the slug hit Flash his body seized and caused him to fire a round into his midsection.

"Good! Motherfucka!" Renee screamed at the dead man, giving him a kick in the face for good measure. Killa thought about shooting her too as she fumbled to remove the money out the dead man's pocket. Instead he smiled.

"Here!" said thrusting a bloody hundred dollar bill towards Killa. "I don't sell no pussy!" she insisted. "You hear that, motherfucka! I don't sell no pussy!" she yelled again at the dead man, kicking him again.

"Yo, ma, we need to get up out of here," Killa said pulling her away. "I need a spot to chill."

"I got a place, come on!" she replied coming up with Flash's keys. They got into his car and hit the highway with the girl driving. "My cousin got a place in Cobb County that no one know about, we can stay there," she announced.

Again Killa entertained killing her, but he needed her. He was thirty-eight hot and once police ran the prints it would only make matters worse. He needed a place to lay low until it was safe enough to travel. He also needed money. A lot of money.

"I see you," Renee announced. "I'm straight! I ain't gone tell on you. Shit, you did me a damn favor! That nigga, my own damn cousin put me on the street to sell my ass! My own gotdamn momma put me out for smoking some weed! Shit, Shawty, you saved me. I ain't gone tell."

"How safe is this place?" he asked cautiously.

"Very! He only use it as a stash spot. Nobody know where it is. He only took me there to rape me!" she spat. A single tear escaped her eye and ran down her cheek. Killa caught it as it feel from her face.

"Check, ma, we need each other," he said sincerely. "I gotta get some money in a hurry. What he got stashed at this place?"

"Lots," she said pulling into an upscale apartment complex.

Chapter 23

Her *lots* turned out to be a little under five thousand dollars. Killa shook his head while he counted it. "Here put this with it," she offered holding out a couple hundred more bloody dollars.

"You keep that," he replied. "Might wanna wash that off too."

Renee laughed and Killa again noticed her. She was young but had an old soul. Put him in the mind of Lisa, Fatimah and Monique all rolled into one.

It was time for a tear to escape his eye as memories flooded his mind. Everyone he cared about died. Not only did they die, he killed them. Directly or indirectly he caused their death. Every one of them would be alive today if they had not met him. Even his mother.

"What's wrong?" Renee asked joining him on the sofa. "I know you ain't tripping 'bout Flash?" she said comforting him. "I know you ain't never killed nobody before and it got you fucked up but my cousin would have killed you. Me too, maybe. You did the whole world a favor."

"Yeah, I never did that before," Killa said pulling her close. "I feel so, so... scared," he said fighting not to laugh.

"It's okay, baby," she purred laying his head on her rather large breasts. Killa lifted up her shirt and removed one from the frilly laced bra.

"Mmm hmm," she said as he took her nipple into her mouth. "That's right baby. Renee got you. I'ma make you feel better."

Killa reached under the small skirt and played in her wetness. As he did she fumbled to remove his belt and free his dick.

When she had him free from his pants she mounted him and worked him inside.

"Mmm… you so tight," he said as she squeezed down on his dick.

"Cuz, I've been saving it for you, baby," she lied and began rocking back and forth. Killa didn't even think about the condom until he began coming inside of her. "That's right, daddy, let me get that!" Renee chuckled.

He wasn't finished with her though. Without even pulling out, he got up and carried her into the plush bedroom and over to the king sized bed. Killa put her thick thighs on his shoulders and plunged deep inside of her.

He pounded her savagely and she loved it. They both reached a breathtaking orgasm and collapsed into each other.

"We straight now?" she asked in between gulps of air. She didn't buy that first time bullshit he spit at her one bit. He was a killer and she knew it. He was also just the right one to take care of her. Just the right one who wouldn't take advantage of her.

"Yeah, we cool," he replied as sleep overwhelmed him. He had no choice but to trust her as he drifted off.

When Killa's mind awoke the next morning he hesitated at opening his eyes. He was afraid. Afraid of the unknown. Instead he allowed his other senses to explore his surroundings.

His ears processed the music playing softly in the next room, while his nose examined the aroma of bacon and possibly biscuits, the ones out the can.

The throbbing in his dick reminded him of the vigorous sex he'd had all night and caused a smile to spread across his face. Finally, he opened his eyes and took in the plush room that was home, for now.

"Hey baby," Renee sang as she entered the room with a plate piled high with steaming breakfast. "I ain't know what you liked, so I made some of everything."

"Killa looked at the tall, well-built girl and again was glad he hadn't kill her. Then he hoped he wouldn't have to.

"Thanks!" he said accepting the plate and digging in. "Mmph," he nodded approvingly at the fluffy spoonful of almost orange cheesy eggs. He followed it up with simultaneous bites of bacon and the biscuit.

"You remember you said we need to get some money," she purred watching proudly as he devoured the food. "Well," she continued without waiting for a response. Not needing to. She'd been online earlier that morning. She knew who was sleeping in her bed. "I know a couple niggas that got more money than they need."

"So what, you wanna take it from them?" Killa chuckled amused by the suggestion and giddy from the wonderful food. "Where you learn to cook like this?"

"My grandma. Now stop changing the subject," she demanded causing him to look up at her. "You wanna get some money or what?"

"I'm listening," he said turning his attention back to his plate of food.

"Okay, well, like I said my ex that nigga got a little money and chumped me off. Nigga wouldn't even let me stay with him when I got put out," Renee said getting more animated as she went on. "I go over there with my bags, and mind you this nigga just fucked me the night before, and now he got some bitch on the sofa and..."

"He got money? Real money?" Killa asked in an attempt to cut what was sure to be a long story short.

"Well, he got four cars, two houses, a bunch of jewelry," she replied. Killa chomped on a biscuit not moved. None of that spelled money.

"Oh, he got like twenty or thirty stacks in that little safe," she added going into another long winded tirade. "That nigga kill me! He got all that money yet bought the cheapest safe they had! I was with him and was like baby..."

Meanwhile, Killa was stuck back at twenty or thirty grand. It wasn't like the licks he was use to but it was a start. He had no plans on running around broke like a desperado. He planned to stack up then go on the run. Most fugitives got bagged by being broke and desperate. Eric Rudolph got caught eating out of a garbage can like a damn raccoon.

"How can I get next to him?" Killa asked cutting off the narrative again. "Shit, that ain't no problem!" she exclaimed. "Stupid nigga called me this morning talking 'bout some, let me hit it. I'ma let him hit it all right."

"Shit, we can get him," Killa said eager to get back to work. "Matter fact, let me hit!"

"Come on! Renee laughed and pulled off his t-shirt she was wearing. She climbed back in the bed and Killa fucked her like it was the last time he was gonna get to hit it. That was just in case, just in case he had to kill her!

After sexing her thoroughly they carefully plotted out the lick. They spent the next week watching his every move. When the time was right they made their move...

Chapter 24

Xing Lee was talking cash shit as the good doctor stroked away at her hairless box. She was 'oohing' and 'aahing' and cursing in her native tongue as her current lover loved her. For all he knew she was talking bad about him but he didn't speak Vietnamese so it sounded as good as it felt.

"Me love you long time!" Doc grunted as he slammed into her. His love life had greatly improved since his miserable wife had been killed by the hands of one of the country's most dangerous killers known as Killa.

The doctor was treated as a hero after surviving the home invasion that claimed his beloved wife. A minor celebrity to all except his wife's family. They blamed him for his former patient taking her life.

Doc now had quite a few girlfriends on payroll, but Xing was by far his favorite. He currently had her on her side in the 'scissor' position and was giving her the business. He was four and a half inches deep pounding away. His prim and prissy wife would have never let him put her in a position like this. Whenever she did feel benevolent enough to part with a little vagina it was one way. From the back while laying on her side so she wouldn't have to look at him. There was no kissing, no talking or tenderness. Just hurry up and get off and get off.

When the doctor's stroke grew choppy Xing threw it into overdrive. She began moaning and thrashing around as if he was slaying it. He wasn't, she was just a good actor. Her performance helped doc reach an intense orgasm he no doubt would tip for.

Xing was bright enough to at least let her lover think he was knocking it out the park. The key to a man's heart is his ego, not stomach. Any stranger can fill your belly, but making a middle aged man feel vibrant was more important. She may or may not have had an orgasm along with him. It's hard to tell with professionals, or wives.

"Ooh, Doctor, you number one G.I! You love me long time!" Xing said quite believably as she got up from the bed. She rushed into the bathroom and under the shower. She was back minutes later and quickly dressed. A kiss on the forehead served as goodbye and she was gone.

"I'm an animal!" Doc cheered, beating on his chest like King Kong. It's one of the silly things people do when they think they're alone, only he wasn't.

"Lion or tiger?" a voice asked from the shadows.

Ordinarily the ordinary man would have been frightened at the presence of an uninvited stranger in his home but he wasn't. He actually smiled at the sound of the voice he knew well. Uninvited he may have been, but he was no stranger.

"A lion. I'm king of the fucking jungle!" he laughed as his now welcome guest stepped from the shadows and into view. "How long have you been here?"

"Long enough to see you and your buddy bumping uglies. Oh, and I speak Korean. She was saying you have a little dick and your elbow was pulling her hair."

"Fuck you, Killa! She's Vietnamese," Doc laughed, cracking them both up. "Let me put something on."

Killa turned away when the doctor bounded out of the bed in his pinkish birthday suit.

"You're looking trim. No homo," he complimented.

"None taken, thank you," Doc said proudly as he headed into his bathroom to wash his and Xing's body fluids off of him. When he returned he found the room empty. He almost called out in fear until he smelled his guest in the other room. Killa had found his way to the den and poured a shot of cognac to go along with his blunt. Doc found him laying back in a recliner blowing smoke rings from the pungent weed.

"So, what brings you back to town? I assumed you would be in Brazil or Belize by now. It's been what, a year?" the doctor asked as he poured a shot of his own.

"Back? Shit, I never left. I love Atlanta," Killa replied. He extended the blunt to his host out of courtesy and to his surprise the doctor took it and took a healthy pull.

"A lot's changed," Killa said noting the new life in the older man.

"Well yeah! I've changed everything," the doctor replied between tokes. He assumed Killa meant the new decor of the house not his new demeanor. The weight loss, the tan, the, weed smoking it took his wife's death for him to live.

"I feel like a new man, I'm alive!" Doc cheered.

"Yeah well, murder will do that. Why you think I'm always so fucking happy?" Killa chuckled.

"Been killing much?" Doc asked enthusiastically.

"Have I!" he shot back animatedly at the gross understatement.

"Tell me about. Please!" the doctor gushed eagerly and adjusted himself to get comfortable for the ride. He leaned back on his chaise to enjoy the story totally unaware he would be a part of it.

Chapter 25

"After I escaped from custody I hooked up with this young chick named Renee. She put me on a couple of licks that had wet my whistle for armed robbery stuff. That shit is addictive especially robbing someone who really deserves it."

"I thought her young as was gonna fuck me to death! I swear little mama was insatiable. She wanted it every few minutes. I felt like a monkey. Still I hated it when she passed."

"Passed? How did she die?" Doctor asked leaning forward.

"Got shot, and no I didn't shoot her."

There was no need for any fancy smancy machine because the killer's emotions were visible on his sleeve. He was genuinely sad.

Their first robbery together was textbook. It worked like a charm. Another silly dealer so caught up with his Rep and status that he got too comfortable.

Renee's ex-boyfriend Reef thought with his dick instead of brain and now it was gonna cost him. He thought he was such a player that he could do or say anything to his women. Reef dissed Renee when she got put out of her home for smoking weed and wouldn't put her up. He fucked her one last time and put her out. That's how she ended up in the clutches of her pimping- cousin the late Flash. And that's how she ended up with Killa.

It only took a couple of days before Reef missed Renee's tight spot. He casually called her and requested a booty call as if nothing had happened. She cursed him out and declined until the plan to rob him was developed.

Killa spent the next week watching his every move while Renee courted him via telephone. His surveillance revealed that the reckless dealer liked pizza and pussy. It was time to make a special delivery.

Reef was such a freak he had Renee play in her pussy over the phone every night. At least he thought she was, in fact she would hold the phone to her mouth as she rode Killa. When she yelled she was cumming, she really was.

"We got him now, daddy," Renee said when she hung up. "He wants me to spend the night with him. He said I can order any kind of pizza I want."

Killa watched, parked half a block away in a rental car, as Renee got dropped off in a cab at Reef's house. The silly man pulled the door open without even checking to see who it was or who was with them.

A minute later his cell phone rang and he smiled at the pretty picture of a parted vagina on the caller ID screen as he answered.

"Sup, lil mama, how we look?"

"Ah...yes, I want to order a pizza and some wings," Renee replied, still sticking with the script, which meant Reef was in her face. "I want the biggest you have."

"Big like my dick?" Killa laughed.

"Mmm...that is big. I can't wait to get that in my mouth," she purred causing Reef to frown. "And twenty wings too please."

"Any guns anywhere insight or anyone else in the house?" Killa inquired cautiously.

"Um... no just enough for two," she replied letting him know that they were alone. *"Wow, that soon?"*

"They said ten minutes," She said as she tried to fend off Reef's eight hands. She had once loved this man with her whole heart, but now she hated his guts. He'd thrown her to the wolves and a wolf raped and pimped her.

"Shit, that's enough time for me to get my dick sucked!" he cheered triumphantly as if he had just won a medal. Which is understandable because good head is like winning a tournament or election. It's the same.

"I gotta pee!" Renee said pushing his dick away from her face. She got up and bolted to the bathroom where she intended to wait.

Killa waited several minutes, watching the surroundings before moving. He donned his makeshift pizza man disguise and pulled to a stop in front of the house. As he approached he scanned the block for police and witnesses. He reached into the pizza delivery bag and clutched the sawed off shotgun inside and tapped on the door with this free hand.

"Who?" Reef barked as he pulled the door open. Not who and then check before opening, and that was going to cost him dearly. Death had just crossed his threshold.

Just before Killa's patented killer smile had a chance to spread on his handsome face a sudden distraction changed the plans. A loud throttling sports car with a loud paint job and a loud stereo whipped up to the house. Out jumped a loud mouth gold toothed having man wearing a loud purple shirt.

"Hey, cuz!" he cheered as he practically ran up the walk and steps. Before Killa knew it he was in the house behind him. Since he had nothing but heat in the hot box he pulled it out.

"Yo, Barney, close the door!" he ordered the intruder before turning to his victim. "Reef put your hands in air!"

Reef asked, "Who are you? How you know my name?" He was concerned with the wrong thing. Renee heard the commotion from the bathroom and came out to 'investigate'.

"Oh my!" she said so smoothly Killa would have bought it if he didn't know any better.

"You, go empty his safe and bring me all the money!" he directed sending Renee rushing to comply.

"The fuck going on, cuz?" the guest complained.

"Be easy, shawty," Reef replied as he eased his hand between the cushions where a .357 magnum lived. "That bitch set me up."

"Yep!" Killa laughed as he pretended not to see him going for his gun.

"Put your hands on your head while you still have one!" Killa demanded.

The Initial plan was to tie Reef up and leave them alive. It was him who chose death over losing his money. In the split second it took for Killa to glance over at Renee who just returned to the room Reef made his move.

It was a silly move with a shotgun pointed at your face. Reef made a play for the gun but came up short as Killa bought death to his life. A quick tug on the trigger caused the big gun to bark. The huge slug hit Reef square in his Adams apple and almost decapitated the man. His cousin screamed so loudly and shrilly that both Killa and Renee looked around to make sure a woman wasn't present in the room. With nothing to lose and his life to gain the man made a desperate lunge for the front door. The shotgun opened a hole in his back big enough to see through but didn't kill him.

"Dang!" Renee giggled at the carnage, making Killa proud. He knew he had found a good one. Most chicks don't have the stomach for that part of the game. They stepped over the bodies and made their escape to their suburban hideout.

"I shoulda shot that dude one more time," Killa said wistfully. "When I saw all that daylight through him I figured he was dead. I figured wrong and paid for it."

"How? What happened?" Doc asked sitting straight up. "Did he follow you? Did he…"

"Chill, Doc. I'm getting to it," Killa laughed despite the sorrow. Had the machine been running it would have certainly registered the regret. But Doc didn't need it, he knew the man well enough to feel him.

"Okay. Roll another blunt thingy and I'll whip up something to eat," Doc offered.

Chapter 26

"That wasn't half bad," Killa exclaimed after polishing off the last bit of food from his plate. "For white people food that is."

"White people food! What the hell is white people food?"

"Goat cheese omelet with figs and wheat germ shake," Killa replied repeating the menu.

"Sorry, I was fresh out of grits and hog maws!" Doc laughed. "What the hell is a hog maw anyway?"

"Hell if I know! Only part of a pig I ever touched was a football."

"Okay, so tell me what happened to your girlfriend," Doc asked settling back into his chair.

"Well, we got back to our spot to count the money and..."

"I thought you said dude had money!" Killa lamented as they emptied the bag on the bed.

"He did!" Renee cheered at the sight of the most money she'd ever seen.

"This is a bunch of change!" he said at the pile of fives and tens. "You don't need a safe for this, you can carry this in your pocket!"

It was yet another case of a nigga flashing cash to impress some chick. Flashing cash can get you some ass but can also get you in a casket, as it did in this case.

"So, I didn't do good?" Renee pouted sticking her bottom lip out which made Killa hard instantly.

"You did great, ma," he said gently and laid her on top of the cash on the bed. He peeled off her little panties and played in her private parts for a few minutes before diving inside.

A half hour later when he slumped over on top of her out of breath he was perfectly content with the haul. 'Fuck it' they would just catch another baller slipping.

Being on the run was expensive so Killa needed to strike again immediately. He also had to be extremely careful, because one slip up meant a lethal injection. His first potential target was the Weed Man. He was selling ounces of exotic herbs at five hundred a pop so he should be sitting pretty.

Only problem was Killa liked the dude. Not to mention he got his weed from him. How are you supposed to stay high if you kill the Weed Man?

"That's the thing about robbing, Doc, you have to kill them. Ain't no coming back and catch a nigga sleeping. Catch you watching a movie and John Wilkes Booth you!" Killa said breaking in on the doctor's mind movie.

"Interesting euphemism," Doc nodded at the presidential reference.

"Figured you would appreciate it," Killa laughed.

"Word!" Doc exclaimed almost sounding hip, almost. "So who did you get?"

"Some nigga who was just begging to get murdered. I was gonna kill him on the strength, robbing him was an afterthought!" Killa growled.

"Why? What he do? Chump you off?" the Doctor inquired excitedly. He leaned back onto his chair preparing for another murderous narrative.

"Renee was technically still a kid and loved movies. Me, I'm more of an intellectual and prefer to study…"

Even though Killa was one of America's most wanted, Renee was still able to coax him into taking her to a movie. They selected the most popular theater so there would be a large crowd to blend into.

Only problem was that Renee was a bad bitch and attracted lots of attention. She could turn heads wearing a potato sack, so the short yellow skirt could not be ignored. All men, alone or with wives and children gawked. Only one was disrespectful enough to try to holla at the obviously taken woman.

"Say, shawty! Shawty! Let me holla at you!" a voice called out from behind them. Assuming he had to be talking to someone else Killa and Renee kept walking.

"You in the yellow!" he called again surprising and confusing the couple.

Renee looked down to see if her dress really was yellow and Killa checked to see if he had become invisible. They both turned to see a flashy Playa-Playa type in a new coupe. It was only the brand new Audi that prevented him from being murdered on the spot. His big mouth almost ruined all these nice people's evening.

"I think he wants to donate all his money to our cause," Killa chuckled and gently pushed her forward. Renee knew

163

what time it was and turned on the charm. *"Get all his info, ma."*

"Come on, shawty, that nigga ain't hitting on shit!" the driver urged. *"Let a real player holla at ya!"*

"Sup handsome," Renee purred seductively as she leaned into his hundred thousand dollar car.

"Sup with you?" he shot back reaching around to palm her ass under the short skirt. When he got no resistance he slipped a finger under her panties and inside of her. *"Damn, you wet already! Must be feeling a nigga!"*

Renee fought the urge to laugh when he sucked the *"wetness"* off his finger trying to be sexy. She knew Killa had just came in her a few minutes ago before they left the house.

"Mm...how it taste, daddy?" she asked, biting her tongue so she wouldn't laugh.

"Sweet, lil mama. Taste like pineapple. You need to hop in so I can take you somewhere and suck that pussy inside out!" he offered then grimaced to show off his platinum teeth, much like a peacock spreading its feathers. *"Oh yeah, my name Dap."*

"Okay Dap, gimme your number and I'll call you," Renee ordered.

"Aight, shawty," he said and slipped a finger back in her and ate a little more cum as she wrote down his digits. He stared Killa down like he was doing something as he pulled off still sucking his finger. He did something alright, disrespected the most dangerous man on the planet.

"I may not even kill him," Killa laughed, "Just tell him what he was eating instead."

"See, daddy, told you pineapple juice makes you taste sweet. Even he liked it. Now when you gonna do me?" she whined.

"Huh? You're breaking up. I lost the signal. Oh, the movie 'bout to start," Killa laughed avoiding the question again. She had been begging him to go down on her, but he wasn't hearing it.

Dap obviously planned on making robbing him as easy as possible. From their first conversation he offered Renee everything he could think of. He could technically be named as an accessory to the pending crime.

Dude actually talked until he was out of breath telling her all of his business. He gave up his whole operation in an hour. All she got out was 'Hey, this is Renee' when he took the call.

When he bragged about his crib she asked for pictures which he gladly sent. Of course he slipped in a few pictures of his dick as well. Pussy has its highest value before you get it so he went all out at the prospect of new pussy. Once you hit it, no matter how good it is, it goes in the pile with the other used vaginas. Of course if it's extra good, does tricks, or has special powers it gets placed on the top of the pile.

Killa, meanwhile went high tech and pulled satellite pictures of the house and figured out all the angles. Once Dap bragged about his security system Killa researched that as well. In minutes he found a way to bypass it in seconds.

Playing hard to get for a month drove stock in Renee vagina to an all-time high. The time was right for either an ISO or robbery. Dap was so eager to fuck, when Renee told him she wanted it on top of a hundred grand he laid out that much on his bed and sent the pictures. After fucking her man real good Renee went on her date.

While she dined on food she couldn't pronounce Killa hopped his back fence from the surrounding woods. He was amazed at how accurate his Intel was. He navigated around like if he lived there. In seconds he rendered the alarm system useless and was in.

The inside of the home was laid out exactly as the blueprints he obtained from the tax assessor's office said it would be. Killa walked through the house as if he had grew up in it. As he walked he pulled up the YouTube video showing how to crack the safe at the idiot had showed off.

"Fuck outta here!" he laughed as he saw all the cash spread on the bed and the safe open wide.

Dap had planned to make good on his promise to fuck her on top of a hundred grand. He could have easily swept the money into his bag and been gone. Had it not been for the disrespect he would have. No, Dap was going to have to pay for that. Which was gonna be hard to do without any money. Besides they had yet to print that much money yet.

Killa's phone buzzed to alert him of an incoming text message. "Skipping movie. Be there in a half hour."

To kill time Killa flipped on Dap's TV. The screen filled instantly with a pretty vagina that made Killa sit still. He watched as a finger made little circles that made the owner of the box whimper.

The camera pulled back allowing the owners pretty face to be seen distorting as she came. The light skin pretty girl was just Killa's type, thick!

Right after she came Dap came in to view and dropped his face into her crotch. "Eww," Killa grimaced as he lapped at her vagina, even though he was strangely curious.

"Ole boy got a mean tongue game. Let him eat you when you get here," Killa tapped out on his phone.

"LMAO you nasty! He already begging to eat it," Renee texted back.

When Dap stood to enter the woman Killa turned it off. Oddly he didn't want to see that. Instead he took the DVD out and tossed it in his bag. When they arrived a few minutes later he ducked into a closet and raised his gun.

Dap extended his life a few more minutes by not coming into the closet. Instead he laid Renee on the money and dove headfirst under her skirt.

"Mmm...this pussy sweet!" he exclaimed between slurps.

"That's that pineapple juice again," Renee replied trying not to laugh. "My man be drinking it."

"You must have drunk some too cause this box is sweet!"

"Un uh, he came in me before I came over!" Renee managed on the verge of an unexpected orgasm. The slow man had a quick tongue and made her cum just as his mind finally caught up.

"What you mean, shawty?" he asked with his face practically dripping. *The look on his face caused her to crack up, good thing Killa was there to answer.*

"She means I just bust a nut in her an hour ago. You a nasty dude, son," Killa replied with his gun by his side.

Dap looked back and paused to process what was going on. Once he got it he made a move for the .40 Cal on his nightstand as Killa shook his head. He grabbed it and did a roll on the ground like a corny cop movie and came up firing. Well, came up clicking cuz the gun was empty.

"Looking for these, stupid?" Killa asked showing him an open palm full of shells.

"Who are you? What do you want?" he moaned as a *single tear ran down his cheek. Funny thing is that this was the same dude who was just beefing with someone online. He had just posted some real tough talk earlier today. Had the cap locks on and everything. Typing real hard, but now, under the gun he was whining.*

"Wow, you are stupid," Renee said as she got up. *For good measure she mushed him as she passed by.*

"Well, for starters that's only twenty five grand. I believe you told my girl something about a hundred stacks," Killa answered.

"Well, see..." Dap began as he tried to explain, *but what was there to explain? He was fronting.*

He, like a lot of dope boys, spent so much money on frivolous shit he was cash poor. They may rock icy jewels and push hot wheels, but between tricking and re-ups niggas ain't have no real dough. If you can't walk in your safe, you ain't really holding dough.

"Look, it's okay, homey," Killa comforted. "Maybe they got traps in the afterlife. You can get your weight up then."

"Afterlife? That's for dead people!" Dap said really crying now.

"Now see, I don't like this Dap. I like the disrespectful motherfucker we met at the movies. Where is that fly ass mouth now?" Killa asked using his boot as a question mark.

In a classic example of worrying about the wrong thing Dap went after the few platinum teeth removed by the kick. For it he got another kick right in the seat of his pants.

"Chill shawty! I can put you on a real nice lick!" Dap pleaded. "My man, Dallas, got that check for real!"

"See how easy niggas give niggas up?" Killa asked his girl. "Bet this nigga would sing like Neyo if the police ever get him in an interrogation room."

"Please, shawty, please!" Dap begged crawling towards his killer as he screwed a long silencer onto his pistol. "I'll do anything! Please, don't kill me!"

"Someone has to pay for that disrespect. Tell you what, either you or your mother. One of you gotta die," Killa hissed as Renee looked around the room for stuff dead people didn't need. You would think he would have at least took a second to think but he didn't.

"My mama done lived her life! Kill her, she old anyway!" he blurted shocking the man who blew up a whole funeral *home while a funeral for two people he blew up was being held. "She stay at..."*

"Pst'...pst'...pst'," the nine whispered like it had a secret as it sent slugs into Dap's inner thoughts.

"Give...pst'...up...pst'...your...pst'...own...pst'...mother! Pst'...pst'...pst'...pst'...click...click. Faggot ass nigga!" Killa growled as he emptied the gun in him. When he ran out of bullets he started kicking the body.

"Wow! What got into you?" Doc asked bringing him back into the present. Now he wished he did have his program running. The scientist in him would have loved to see what that looked like on his screen.

"I don't know, Doc, but that shit enraged me. Maybe I'm getting soft," he offered slightly embarrassed. "Shit, if you think that was bad wait 'til the end of the story. That's when it really gets ugly!"

Doc beamed internally, he liked ugly.

Chapter 27

"A-yo doc, what you got to eat up in here?" Killa asked breaking the spell.

"Eat? I...... shit, I am kinda hungry," he admitted once he saw how much time had elapsed. "I got something special. Come on, I'll hook you up yo!"

"Hook up, yo?" Killa laughed as he once again followed his buddy into the kitchen.

"Roll up!" Doc ordered as he began removing items from the fridge and cupboards. "We'll blaze one after we eat".

"Well, since I was technically *on the run*," Killa began, making quotation signs with his fingers. "I didn't venture out much during the day. For the most part all we did was fuck, smoke, sleep and fuck."

Actually Renee did most of the sleeping while Killa studied. After dicking his young partner in crime to sleep he would scour the internet in search of knowledge and information. His favorite subject was how to kill.

He read up on all of America's so-called serial killers and scoffed. He had more bodies than all of them. They had nothing on him. It was the notorious hitmen who really caught his attention. His own uncle, Cameron Forrest, was said to be one of the most prolific killers in the profession.

Killa wasn't sure what to believe. He knew firsthand how far out of proportion legends could be. Take the rumor of him blowing up a funeral home and killing 100 people. Well, he did blow up a funeral home, while the funeral was in process for some people he'd blown up, but only sixty nine people died in the blast.

He also went high tech; studying alarm systems and safe cracking. He quickly found out that the movies were full of shit. Using a stethoscope and listening to tumblers will get you nowhere. Most safes now had biometric keys and multiple combinations. That meant cutting off fingers and plucking out eyes, neither of which he had a problem with.

Soon the inactivity begin to get to the both of them. They needed to get out, and live a little, of course they needed some money to live on as well. So Killa went through the late Dap's phone and found the man Dallas he'd spoken of. The one who had that check.

Killa's investigation put his target in a half million dollar subdivision. The satellite confirmed dude was ballin'. He was about to get robbed!

While Killa was in the phone he came across the same girl from the video. "Kitty huh?" he nodded studying her pretty face. He thought about hitting the send button but shook it off.

She was thick just like he liked them. Killa preferred a sixteen to a six any day. He liked his women Queen Latifah-ish big and pretty. "U.N.I.T.Y."

"What you over there singing about baby?" Renee mumbled still groggy from a dick induced coma.

"Our next lick. This one may actually have some real dough," he replied clicking off of the picture.

The little money they took from Reef and Dap came to just under 50 grand. Killa figured he would need at least two hundred to disappear with. He may have been on the run but he wasn't running. Being broke and desperate would get you caught.

Not to mention Killa had a pretty expensive weed habit. He smoked five hundred dollar ounces of purp, kush, or dro in 3 days. Then Renee loved shopping almost as much as she did sex. Not quite, but almost.

Yeah he needed a good lick and this dude Dallas may be just the ticket. He began his surveillance by driving by the large house a couple times a day. The running video camera allowed him to do a casual pass then review the footage in detail later. It was far more productive than driving slowly past and staring.

He also contacted the builder listed at the front of the upscale subdivision and obtained the blueprints. A call to the security company whose signs adorned Dallas's plush green lawn provided helpful information as well. They gladly gave up their most popular option plans. Killa wisely assumed he had a total package. With his new found knowledge he could bypass it in seconds.

The beautiful woman seen using her keys to enter ruled out siccing Renee on him and the small child also presented a challenge, but if worse came to worse he would kill the woman and eat the child because dude was coming off that cake.

Calls to the various safe manufacturers and installers also gave up his secrets. Dallas had a state of the art job that cost fifty grand by itself. It was built into the concrete wall in the basement. She took a retina scan, finger print, and a numeric code to spread her legs and give up her booty. There would be no cracking it, Dallas would have to open it.

His movements spelled high level drug dealer. Duffle bags in and duffle bags out said he was dumb. Whatever he was doing, he was doing it around his family.

The little girl reminded him of his own daughter and pushed tears from wherever they come from. He caught one and stared at it oddly. It was the first time he could remember crying ever. Strangely it felt good. It meant he was indeed human because monsters don't cry.

"Baby, can we please go to the club tonight?" Renee asked kneeling in front of her man. Knowing him like she did she relocated his penis from his pants to her mouth knowing he wouldn't say no. "Please!"

"Sure," Killa moaned surprising them both. It may not have been the wisest thing to do, but he like pleasing his girl; especially with the way she was working her hand, lips, and tongue in perfect harmony to please him.

"So, you really went clubbing while on Georgia's most wanted list?" Doc broke in.

"Yeah, good head will do that to you," Killa laughed even though he was serious.

The doctor could relate since Xing recently sucked a car payment out of him only days ago. Women should realize a blow job will get you a lot further than nagging. Wanna see some results? Blow your man! No man gets some good head and says, "I'll be back." If anything he'll want to cuddle.

"Doc, I had a foreboding feeling from the time we left our spot..."

Killa wanted to change his mind and stay in, but Renee was too excited. Of course she would have pouted a bit but once he laid some pipe she would have been fine. Which is a note to fellas: stop bickering. If your woman is suddenly irate or whiny, don't argue. Throw that D!

"How about this?" Renee asked bursting from the walk in closet. She did a little twirl showing off the tiny little skirt she selected.

"I think I'm gonna have to kill somebody if you wear that," he joked with his eyes glued to her fine young figure.

"Perfect then!" she giggled and went back into the closet to pick the rest of her outfit. *"Oh, and when we get home, its pony express time!"*

Killa felt himself stiffen at the mention of his favorite position. When Renee mounted him she really did try to ride him to California. The promise of sex made him ignore his instincts, something he never did. He was going to pay for it.

Since it was other people's money Killa didn't mind splurging with it. He had rented a new drop top coupe to ride in. Renee was killing shit in her red mini dress but Killa wasn't doing too bad himself.

He rocked a subdued pair of black gators along with a pair of black slacks and charcoal grey button down shirt. His newly acquired short afro was cut to razor sharp perfection.

His caramel skin tone had lightened slightly from not venturing out during daylight hours. That's one of the drawbacks of life on the run. While he didn't go out much during the day, Killa ruled the night. This was the time he moved freely about, as if he wasn't a wanted man. He may have been on the run, but he wasn't hiding. He had a bushy patch of chin hair that could be called a goatee.

Being on the run is not easy. Take it from me. It's no fun on the run. However, Killa was cut from a different cloth. He vowed he would never be apprehended. He was not going back to jail. If and when the law caught up with him it was going down on the spot. Until then he planned to live until he died.

The gorgeous couple made a grand appearance when they pulled up to the upscale club on Peachtree Street in the heart of down town Atlanta. Guys sweated her starting from her mile long legs leading to her perfectly round ass. Her flat stomach and fat breast also made an impression on the way to her beautiful face and blinding smile.

Meanwhile the girls swooned over the 6'1" killer from the Bronx. They posed as he passed hoping for eye contact. Most assumed he was a celebrity or something from his swag. However, not all of the attention was good.

"Say shawty! Say shawty! That's that nigga right there!" Buddah said jumping up and down. His cousin Chase and homeboy Kobe both backed away remembering what happened last time he got too excited in public.

"*Aight shawty, calm down 'fo that bag bust again!*" *Chase said stifling a laugh.*

"*Had shit err where!*" *Kobe cosigned reminding him of last week when he got too active on the dance floor and his colostomy bag dislodged.*

"*That's that nigga that gave me the damn shit bag and kilt yo' brother!*" *Buddah exclaimed.*

"*Who? Where?*" *Chase demanded, looking to where his cousin had pointed, but Killa had already went inside. "That nigga dead!*"

"*Chill shawty! Let's just keep an eye on him and get him when he come out,*" *Kobe wisely suggested. He too wanted to avenge his friend's death, but not out in public. He wasn't trying to catch a murder case.*

"*Nigga put me on a damn shit bag!*" *Buddah whined. When Killa hit him with the shotgun it blew a hole threw him taking important shit like his intestine and spleen out along with it.*

The men took seats at the bar where they could keep tabs on Killa. They hated watching Renee give him a seductive lap dance in the VIP section; that they couldn't get in. They hated all the successful men for being successful.

"*That nigga balling,*" *Kobe complained. "Damn, that bitch fine!*"

"*Probably spending Reef money!*" *Buddah griped and he was right. The money Killa was dishing out so freely had once belonged to the deceased, until Killa took it from him.*

"Come on y'all!" Kobe demanded once the couple stood to leave. Killa had a handful of Renee's ass as they walked right past the danger.

When the valet returned with the rental the men were already locked and loaded. They trailed them onto 75 north and waited. Waited and hated.

They really hated when Renee dropped out of sight into Killa's groin. When the car swerved slightly they knew what was going down. Killa couldn't take it and abruptly whipped over to the shoulder and parked. The maneuver caught them off guard causing them to pass right by.

As they sped up to find the next exit to circle around Renee climbed onto her man's lap. A tug of her wet panties later and she eased down on top of him.

"Couldn't wait huh?" Killa smiled up at her as she found a rhythm and began riding. Quite a few times her firm young body coaxed a quick nut out of him, but this time it was her who suffered from premature ejaculation.

"Oh baby, I'm cumming!" she whimpered and shivered. She came and went at the same time as two slugs fucked up her hairdo.

The impact of the shots knocked her completely off Killa, who took cover. He could only wait as the three men walked up firing. His Sig Sauer was under the seat but had he lifted his head he would have joined Renee, who was staring off into the afterlife.

Then the strangest thing happened. 'Click', 'click', 'click', the three cheap semi-automatics the men carried repeated. He *peeked up into the rearview mirror to confirm the incredible combination of luck and stupidity. Sure enough they had run out of bullets.*

Only Chase had a few more loose bullets in his pocket and scrambled to load them into his gun. He didn't make it. Being the only immediate threat Killa popped up and popped Chase right in his forehead. Kobe was next to go bye-bye because he froze. Funny how hard niggas be until them things start busting. Four upper torso shots made him do the Harlem shake until his body dropped.

Buddah screamed like a bitch, again, as he took off running. His colostomy bag came off leaving a trail of shit as he ran.

"Shit!" Killa spat when his own gun clicked empty. It saved, well, prolonged Buddah's life for a while.

"Oh baby!" Killa moaned at the sight of his dead girlfriend. He didn't have time to mourn. The quick shooting had been witnessed by passing motorists and police were no doubt on the way.

As much as he hated leaving Renee there in the car, he had no choice. After a quick wipe down of all surfaces, he may have touched, he grabbed his extra clip and extra gun and took off. Killa ran through the grass into the woods that lined the express way. He got scratched and tripped over the overgrown vegetation as he ran. Sirens could be heard as police cruisers converged on the area.

Killa peeped out of the woods and spotted a gas station across the street. He looked left, right, and left again just as he was taught as a child; only now he was looking for police cars. The initial plan was to call a cab and flee the area, but God is the best of planners and had something else in store.

"The fuck!" Killa spat when he couldn't find the number for a taxi anywhere on the pay phone. Back in New York there were a million stickers all over the booths. Plan B was out the window as well when he couldn't find a single coin to call information. He was taught that change was for chumps, hence the phrase 'chump change'. Still, the hundred dollar bills in his pocket proved worthless.

"Say shawty, what's happening?" A young goon asked as he pulled his hooptie up beside the phone.

"Check it, I need a ride," Killa replied rushing around to the other side and jumping in. The move initially startled the back seat passenger, but made their plan that much easier. "Drive!"

The driver was a flunky type who was so use to taking orders he immediately complied. He pulled out of the deserted station in the opposite direction. Killa was so eager to flee the area he neither asked questions nor recognized the danger.

"Slipping wasn't you?" Doc broke in.

"Yeah, but they're the ones who paid for it."

"You got some money on gas?" the front seat rider turned and asked. The low budget robbers would have been content with twenty or thirty bucks to smoke on but when Killa recklessly pulled out the roll of hundreds the plan changed.

"Yo, I really appreciate this, here you go," Killa replied handing a c-note to each man. "One for each of you."

"Shit shawty, let me get all that!" the passenger demanded, pulling a cheap pistol. As he attempted to turn and point it Killa sprang into action.

He simultaneously grabbed the gun while pulling his own. Killa pointed the gun at the man next to him and his own at the one in front. The childhood friends died at the exact same moment as both pistols fired small caliber projectiles into their brains.

The driver was so shook up he bailed out the moving vehicle without trying to slow down. He skidded on the concrete street removing all the skin from side of his face. Killa reached up and grabbed the wheel but couldn't reach the brakes. He brought the car to a grinding stop by dragging it along the cars parked on the street.

In an instant he decided no one else was getting away tonight. He climbed over the seat and got behind the wheel. The wounded driver limped up the middle of the street as Killa pulled a New York style U-turn.

When dumb ass saw the car barreling towards him the best his brain could come up with was to limp faster. It wasn't fast enough. The car made the sound of running over speed bumps too fast as it passed over his body, the first time. Killa threw it in reverse and ran him over again and again, and then one more time.

A few dark side streets later Killa was back on Peachtree Street not far from where he started. His luck was a little better and he was able to hail a taxi passing by. Since most taxis operate by dispatch there would be no record of this trip.

Killa

The same three hundred bucks the men chose death for instead of life now kept the African cab driver from turning on the meter.

Killa jumped out the cab blocks from his hideout and hoofed it the rest of the way. As soon as he walked in Renee's lingering perfume filled his nostrils and flushed out his eyes.

"I love you, lil mama!" he finally admitted to her memory. They were words she'd said to him shortly after they met, and every day since.

He plopped down on the sofa and began chain smoking blunts until the sun rose. When he hit the remote the previous night's mayhem dominated the news channels. There had been a near record six homicides that night in the city of Atlanta. Five from his own hands, the sixth his girlfriend.

The reports on the three would be armed robbers gave him some comfort. There's nothing like killing people who really need killing.

"Three men wanted on a violent crime spree were murdered last night in what an unnamed officer calls an Act of Justice. Gerald Lee, Daryl Queen and Sam Little died as violently as they lived. Little and Lee were both shot to death while Queen was repeatedly run over by several vehicles."

"The three men were wanted as prime suspects in several armed robberies and murders. In two of the attacks female victims were sexually assaulted. Including one as young as ten..."

Killa felt a sense of satisfaction knowing he'd done the world a favor. All he had done was take out the trash. Similar

182

reports were given regarding Kobe and Chase. Low-lives the earth didn't need on its surface.

"Doc, I couldn't sleep until I killed that dude," Killa said shaking his head.

"How long did it take you to catch up with him?" Doc asked eagerly.

"About a week, at the funeral. You know how much I like funerals," he laughed.

"You didn't?" Doc questioned, hoping that he had.

"I did, but it was only a little one. It was time to go see Big Shawn for a small bang!"

Chapter 28

Big Shawn started moving guns at age sixteen. He learned the trade from the old heads and had the balls to try it out. Using one thousand crack dollars he boarded the bus from his home in Long Island New York to his grandmother's in Atlanta. His crackhead uncle charged him a buck fifty for each eighty-dollar .380. Back in New York they sold like hotcakes at three hundred dollars apiece. The next trip Big Shawn took along an ounce of Spanish Harlem's finest base and was able to buy twenty guns. That was thirty years ago, soon Big Shawn Bennett was one of the biggest gun dealers in town. Now semi-retired he only had a select few clients and specialized in hard to get exotic weapons. That's exactly what Killa was shopping for.

"I'm Cameron Forrest's people," Killa announced as Bigs opened his door. "Sorry to pop in on you, but my uncle told me good things."

"I see the family resemblance," Big replied as he let him in. They were from different generations and unaware of each other's rep, but both recognized the other as a killer.

"My uncle told me you was the man to see. I need something special," Killa stated as he surveyed the apartment.

"I got or can get anything!" Bigs bragged. Well, it ain't really bragging if it's true and it was. "Follow me."

Killa's knees buckled slightly when he was led into the gun room. In it were weapons, big and small from all over the world. Biggs smiled at the reaction he got so frequently.

"I wanna blow something up." Killa announced almost shyly.

"No problem, I got shit that can knock a house down, or anti personal types to kill fifty, or shape char..."

"Just one. I only wanna blow up one man," Killa said wincing at another stab of compassion that was starting to irritate him. He still planned to brutally murder the man, but just him. No collateral damage.

"This may be what you're looking for," Bigs said holding up a small egg shaped device. "Same shit Denzel used in that movie; the one where he put the bomb in dude's ass."

"Cool," Killa smiled "Only, how does it get in his ass?"

"Or not," Biggs laughed, deciding not to try to explain. "This baby right here will annihilate everything inside of a car and not even break the windows!"

"Say word!" Killa exclaimed as he took the high tech device he'd read about. "Shock, sound, and small high explosive incendiary..."

Now it was Big Shawn's turn to be impressed as Killa accurately explained the latest in murder gear.

"How much?" Killa asked putting the grenade in his pocket.

"On the house, on the strength of your uncle. Just shop with me next time you need some heat."

"That's a bet!" Killa replied. The two men shook hands and Killa turned to leave. He had learned from the death notices that a dual funeral was being held for Chase and Kobe. Killa planned to make it a threesome.

He staked out the funeral home scanning the occupants of each arriving car in search of his prey. His newfound humanity almost went out the window when he saw Buddah pull up with a carload of girls. Had they been men they would have died that day. Died for hanging out with the wrong person, wouldn't have been the first time that's happened. But Killa couldn't bring himself to sacrifice the young women. Two of whom were teens. No, he would wait. He didn't have to wait long.

"Y'all go ahead," Buddah ordered as he pulled up to the funeral home. As the girls piled out he stood up and blew a kiss at one of them from the open sunroof.

Killa smiled at how easy he made killing him and pulled out behind him. He followed from a distance waiting on his opportunity to strike. When Buddah stopped at a light Killa scanned for police. Satisfied that the coast was clear he pulled up alongside.

Killa pulled the pin and tossed it through the sunroof and into his lap. Buddah turned and saw Killa next to him and stomped on the gas pedal. He was more concerned with the killer in the next car than the buzzing steel object between his legs.

Buddah only made it a few feet before the device went off. In an instant all the windows turned red, and pink as the grenade turned him inside out. Then there was a bright flash followed by a blazing fire.

Killa was so happy he actually clapped. "I gotta get more of those!" he thought aloud as he pulled away from the carnage.

"I felt so good after killing that dude that I wanted to celebrate," Killa exclaimed, closing the curtain on the movie playing in the doctor's mind.

"I can totally relate. After... I...my... wife, you know," Doc stammered.

"After you killed your wife," Killa stressed. "Say it. Own it. It'll make you feel better."

"After I killed that miserable cunt! I felt the happiest I had felt in a long time! I went out dancing," Doc admitted. "I...I....want to do it again!"

"You may just get your chance. Soon."

Chapter 29

The security cameras in the gated property meant Killa's pizza man routine wasn't going to fly. It took weeks of researching, waiting, and watching before he finally found a way in. Realizing it could be his last night on earth, if things didn't go right, he decided to go out dancing himself.

Killa smoked a blunt while he watched the video of Kitty playing in her pussy. The next thing he knew his erection was throbbing in his hand.

"Whoa! Killa, I'm sure I don't wanna hear this part!" Doc announced disgusted.

"Chill, Doc, and just listen."

He ended up in a small club off Piedmont Road where spoken word was spoken. It really wasn't his type of scene/crowd but he wasn't in the mood for loud music either. The popular clubs had a bunch of wannabe ballers that made him sick to his stomach. Both men and women pretending to be people they weren't. Of course that's the purpose, but Killa didn't get out enough to understand that.

Club Badu was one of those afro-centric type spots that catered to a Bohemian crowd; the chicks with no perms, who were slightly musty because they didn't believe in deodorant, had hairy legs, and dreads that they cared for with honey and berries and shit.

Killa walked in and wrinkled his handsome face at the musty smell. There wasn't a single weave in the joint. He wasn't sure if these all natural chicks fucked on the first night but be was about to try.

He immediately felt overdressed in slacks and silk shirt. Everyone else was dressed super casual. Guys had on old jeans and sandals and girls wore vintage dresses showing off their hairy legs.

Killa sauntered over to the bar to get a much needed drink. He scanned the darkened room in search of the delightful delicacy known as new pussy. Everything new is great! New cars have the new car smell. New clothes have that fresh crispness to them, but new pussy! Nothing, absolutely nothing beats new pussy!

"Vodka and pineapple," Killa ordered when the barefoot bartender looked his way. He could tell from the look on her face that some bullshit was coming.

"Alcohol is haram! We only serve natural drinks," she implored.

"Haram? I'm not Muslim, that's the dude who writes me. Give me a drink!" Killa shot back.

"Can I have a shot of almond milk with a honey chaser? Make it a double, one for my friend too please," a waif thin yet very pretty woman asked as she stepped to the bar. The bartender turned to fill her order as she turned to Killa to flirt.

"Hotep," she smiled holding a hand up and bowing slightly making Killa laugh.

"Peace Ma," he replied sizing her up for his bed. He was horny but she was way too small. The woman was like a size one from eating berries and bark.

Their small talk was interrupted when their drinks arrived. Killa and whatever African name she said clinked glasses and sipped their milk.

"The fuck!" Killa spat, spitting the thick, warm fluid across the bar.

"It's good for you," she insisted but Killa wasn't hearing it.

"You drink it then. I'm out," he replied and peeled off.

"Peace my brother," she said sadly to his departing back. She knew the concoction would keep his dick hard for days. Killa missed out. Well, not really.

"I was ready to go home, throw the Kitty video back on and take matters into my own hands. Feel me?"

"I do not, but go on," Doc nodded.

As Killa rode up Peachtree Street he came across a line of pretty women waiting to get into a club. Figuring he'd try his luck again he pulled up front. Using the valet allowed all who saw to see he had a little cake. It was bait, he was hunting bedmates.

The velvet rope was parted at the VIP line as he approached. A c-note laced pound paid the admission and he was in. Killa blinked the dim establishment into view as he walked in. Once he spotted the bar he made a beeline to it.

"Vodka and pineapple!" he ordered eagerly.

"Coming right up," the vested bartender exclaimed just as eagerly. Several seconds later he returned with the drink.

"Rum and coke please," a soft voice said next to Killa as he lifted the drink to his mouth. He almost choked when he saw who it was.

"Kitty?" he smiled at his video crush.

"Yeah, and who are you?" she shot back defensively. "Who are you? Only people who know me, know me, call me Kitty!"

"I um... I'm Ki...I mean, I'm Killa. I met you at Dap's funeral."

"Oh, ok. I'm sorry, I don't remember," she offered sincerely. "Fucked up what happened to him, but he was begging for it."

"How so?"

"He was very disrespectful. Thought his little money meant he could talk to people anyway he wanted to. He was a murder waiting to happen," she replied. "I only showed up out of pity."

"Pity is good. You ever have pity sex?"

"Pity sex? What position is that?" the pretty woman asked playing along.

"You know, meet a lonely handsome stranger and donate some vagina." Killa said struggling not to laugh.

"I think I might tonight, and since your name is Killa you better kill it!" she smiled wickedly.

"Let's bounce!" he said tossing his drink down his throat. Kitty followed suite by draining her glass in one gulp.

"I'll drive," Killa offered once they emerged onto the street. She nodded her approval as the valet took off to retrieve his car.

In the bright lights Killa realized he'd struck gold. Not only was she pretty thick, she was pretty and thick. Her long natural curly hair glistened in the street lights. 'U.N.I.T.Y'

Kitty too was impressed with the smoothed out thug. She was hood enough to understand his swag. He was a rough neck no matter how clean he was tonight.

She gave him her address which he entered into the vehicles navigation system. The twenty minute ride was filled with playful banter laced with sexual innuendo. It was verbal foreplay that had them both peaked.

"You want me to give you some head while we ride?" Kitty as seductively.

"Hell yeah!" Killa cheered swerving slightly from the excitement.

"I would if we weren't here. Now pull behind that Audi," she laughed.

Once inside the swank little condo Kitty led him straight to her tidy bedroom. Since it was established from jump that they were fucking they quickly disrobed.

Killa smiled to himself singing 'U.N.I.T.Y.' at the sight of her peeling off her size 16 dress.

"I have a special request if you don't mind," Killa offered sheepishly.

"Knew you was a freak!" Kitty laughed. *"What, swing from the chandelier?"*

"Well....?" *Killa paused thinking that might be cool too.* *"Nothing too serious, just I need you to play in it for me."* *He wanted a live viewing of the show he'd watched more than he would ever admit.*

"Shit, no problem. I have a request too. Actually it's a prerequisite. I DO NOT, I repeat, I DO NOT fuck unless you eat my pussy!" *Kitty said adamantly.*

"Now see, Doc," Killa interjected pausing the show. "I did not, never had, and never planned on eating pussy!"

"So, what did you do, go back to the club!? Find another? Did you kill her? What?"

"Shit, I ate that pussy!"

"That's wonderful! Pussy is a wonder food! Full of protein with zero calories!" Doc gushed cracking Killa up. He pictured him doing a commercial for it. Holding a sign that read EAT MORE PUSSY!

Killa leaned in tentatively and sniffed, as we do when trying a new food for the first time, which he was. He marveled at how her lips swelled in anticipation.

Fuck it he thought and flicked his tongue at it.

"Mmmmm!" *Kitty moaned as her whole body reacted.*

After a few more cursory licks Killa dove in. Good thing eating pussy is almost self-explanatory. She shifted and moaned alerting him to where, what, and how and he obeyed. He was extremely pleased with himself when she came hard enough to shake the room.

"My turn," he announced with a wet grin as he rolled a condom down his long erection. He moaned as he pushed inside her comfy insides and made himself at home.

He made slow, passionate love to her until she came again. Then Killa fucked her. He lifted her thick caramel thighs and plunged to the bottom. He pounded as if drilling for oil, but found a nut instead.

"Shit!" they said together as he slumped over on top of her. They both were asleep in seconds.

Killa woke up the next morning to Kitty's full lips around his morning erection. Once he was fully up she mounted him and slid down slowly. She rode him to a mutual orgasm that called for breakfast.

"You just earned yourself the Kitty special!" she cheered as she dismounted.

"You mean that wasn't it?" he asked.

"No, silly. I'm finna cook you an omelet!" Kitty laughed.

After showering together to wash off the body fluids they headed into the well equipped kitchen where Kitty kept her promise. She begin pulling out the fixings to fix him a western omelet.

"What do you do, if you don't mind me asking?" Killa asked noticing that the kitchen had every kitchen appliance known to man. Including an expresso maker that he knew cost at least a grand.

"Temp work here and there, but mostly fuck dope boys," she replied, as she chopped and diced vegetables.

"What a coincidence," Killa laughed causing his host to snap her head in his direction.

"How so?" she inquired but was interrupted by a knock on the door saving Killa from having to answer. "Hope that's the damn cable man, my shit been out for a whole day!"

Killa watched as the sexy lady clad only in T-shirt and panties walked to answer the door. Since she was expecting him she didn't bother to ask who it was. She just pulled open the door to let him in.

In an instant Killa had saw his way into the fortress Dallas called home. It was a low tech solution to a high tech problem. All he had to do was knock. Now all he needed was a uniform.

Chapter 30

"I hate heights, Doc. It's not a phobia or anything so don't start analyzing. I'm just saying, don't like being any higher than a good blunt can take me!"

"Fuck!" Killa sighed as he stared up at his destination. The plan, though simple called for him to climb a telephone pole.

The junction box that was his target sat thirty feet high, but to Killa it seemed much higher. A mile or so have him tell it. Still, the promise of what riches waited in that safe urged him on. It had to be a sweet lick. Maybe enough to lay low and live on. Take Kitty to Belize and chill.

Kitty, he chuckled at the thought of the woman. She had texted him earlier letting him know they now 'went together'. He had no objections, 'U.N.I.T.Y.' he sang to himself as he climbed before he knew it he'd arrived.

"Just don't.....shit!" he said shaking his head as he looked down. He quickly shook off his apprehension and got to work.

A quick snip cut the cable to the target house. Just as quickly he tapped directly into the phone line. He was betting that the pretty "kept woman" Dallas kept couldn't go long without cable or internet. She couldn't.

"Cable Company," Killa answered the first call that came from the large home.

"This is 187 Moss Street and my cable is out. I demand that you send someone over this instant!" she fumed.

"We have a driver in the area. He'll be there in a few minutes," Killa said politely.

"Well hurry up!" she spat angrily and hung up. She was the type of woman men loved to kill but were too scared to. Not Killa though. He filled his mind with thoughts of Kitty and made his way back to earth.

A few minutes later he pulled his cable van up to the gate and was buzzed in. He shot a glance to the back of the van where its real driver lay. He was snoring peacefully from the sedative Killa gave him. Not long ago Killa would have put him to sleep permanently with a shot to his head. A glance at the picture of him and his family cosigned his choice. It was that damn conscience again, he hoped it wouldn't get him killed.

He swapped out the unnecessary items in the tool box for the tools of his trade. The pliers and snips were replaced by duct tape and a silencer equipped pistol along with plastic ties that worked better than handcuffs.

The large doors swung open as Killa approached. There stood one of the most beautiful women Killa had ever seen in person. The short designer dress she wore was made sheer by sunlight giving him a perfect view of her fat panty covered crotch.

"I cannot believe you people!" she began, launching into a tirade that did not end. The plan to hold her hostage until Dallas came home and rob him almost went out the window.

Killa made up his mind to murder her now and wait in silence. Then the most adorable toddler toddled in and smiled up at him. *The little girl had just saved her mother's life. Being so cute must be exhausting because the baby climbed on the love seat and passed out.*

The grumpy woman now whispered her abuse as Killa fumbled around behind the TV. *Luckily he didn't have to wait much longer before the heavily jeweled man came in.*

"Hey baby," he said planting a kiss on her full lips as he palmed her ass. *He grabbed her ass so hard it squeezed between his fingers.*

"Hey honey. The cable is out and they sent this idiot and..." *was as far as she got before the guns came out.*

"You, hands where I can see them!" *he ordered Dallas before turning to the woman.* "You, SHUT THE FUCK UP!!!!!"

"Who the fuck are you?" *Dallas demanded like a man use to making demands.*

"I'm the man who is going to kill you, her, the baby, the cat, the dog, those fish, all the plants, and every fucking thing else with a pulse if you don't cooperate," *Killa answered honestly. This is as close to death as one can be and still be breathing. This was closer to death than even being on life support and a greedy relative holding the plug.*

"You bas ..." *the pretty woman fumed as she ran up on Killa. An upper cut Mike Tyson would be proud of finally shut her up.*

"Look man, I got ten grand in my car. You can take that and no problems," *Dallas bargained. Only problem was he was in no position to bargain.*

Killa

"This is going to cost you more than ten grand," Killa replied as he plastic cuffed the sleeping woman's hands behind her back. "Now lay on your stomach."

When Dallas complied he cuffed and gagged him with duct tape. His eyes grew huge as the intruder produced a small hatchet from the toolbox.

"Don't worry this may not even be necessary." Killa said soothingly. "As long as you cooperate I won't have to cut your hands off to open the safe."

Dallas began mumbling and shaking his head furiously so Killa removed the gag so he could speak.

"I ain't got no safe. Plus ain't nothing in the safe. Must be the wrong house!" he rambled lies that didn't quite sync up.

"Look, stupid," Killa said pausing to kick him, "I know about the safe with the retina scan and I'll pop your eye out to bypass it. I know about the fingerprint pad and I'll cut off your hands. I need that code so man up, you lost one!"

"Since you know all that you must know whose money that is then," Dallas said fearfully.

"Yeah, my money now quit playing with me!"

Just then the Pretty Woman woke up and looked around. She sighed a deep sigh of relief that her baby was still sleeping soundly on the sofa.

"Hey, look who's up," Killa said cheerfully as if he didn't just knock her out. "Check it, your man is being difficult. Get me in the safe so I can be on my way. So your child doesn't get hurt."

For a reply she looked to her man to tell her what to do. She had a fly mouth and a sharp tongue but knew her position.

"Don't say shit, Candy! He can't get in. He can take the money we have around the house and go buy some crack or blunts," Dallas said smugly. He knew the state of the art safe could not be cracked. The only way in was through that code and no one had it but him, or so he thought.

"Okay, Mr Dallas, who do I start with? Whose head do I chop off first?" Killa asked. "The girl or the woman?"

Dallas just shrugged like 'whatever' and stayed mute.

"Okay, I'm gonna cut this little girl in half!" Killa growled and lifted the ax above the still sleeping child. "Then your woman."

"Don't make me none, that ain't my kid! My bitch got some good ass head, but you can cut it off and take it with for all I care. I can replace her quicker than the money."

"What the fuck did you just say?" the woman asked in tears. "You would let him kill us to keep your money!"

"I'll holla," he said like it was a joke. Killa resolved then that no matter what happened Dallas had lived his last day yesterday. His ass was dying today!

"16, 39, 8, 12," Candy blurted out. "That's the code!"

"The fuck! You nosey bitch! How the fuck you get my code?" Dallas whined.

"You guys can talk about that later. Son, we need to hit the safe so I don't have to cut you up." Killa broke in.

"There's still one more number. Kill him and I'll give it to you," Candy offered.

"K," Killa shrugged and lifted the pistol to shoot.

"Wait!" she said just before he pulled the trigger. She checked her child before continuing. "Let me give you some of this good head before he goes. I want that to be the last thing he sees."

"That's why I fucked your sisters, all your friends, your aunt...." Dallas said venomously.

"K," Killa replied and duct taped his mouth shut again.

He was hurling insults from behind the gag as Candy sucked Killa off. She swallowed with a loud gulp once they finished.

"Now please kill him!" she pleaded.

Killa removed the gag to see if he was ready to cooperate yet, but he wasn't.

"I fucked the lady at the day care, the clerk at the market, and I'm waiting on that little bitch over there to get a little older so I can fuck her too!" Dallas spat.

Both killer and Candy looked over to where the sleeping girl slept to make sure he wasn't talking about someone else. He wasn't. Candy rushed over and tried to take the pistol from Killa. She wanted to kill him herself.

"Fuck you, her, Obama-care, big bird..." Dallas rambled on.

Killa stood behind Candy and let her take the gun. He stayed close enough to prevent her from turning the gun on him. It was an unnecessary precaution, because she barely had it before firing it at his head. Killa had to pull the gun away to stop her from emptying it. Just in case, he needed to shoot her too.

True to his word Killa hacked off his hand and plucked out his eye. Candy led him to the safe where the bloody body parts granted him partial access to the riches contained inside.

"What's the last number?" Killa demanded as he entered the ones he had.

"Split it with me!" she insisted. They both knew there was a timer that would permanently lock the safe if not opened soon.

"What!"

"The money, split it with me. I got a kid and I can't stay in this house. His mom will put me out, that bitch hates me."

"How much is in there?" Killa demanded.

"A lot so split it with me."

"I'll give you 25 percent killer haggled quickly knowing that time was ticking.

"Deal!" she said extending her hand to shake on it. She scanned his soul through his brown eyes as they shook hands looking for deception. She found none and told her secret. "Five, the last number is five!"

Killa counted out $125,000 dollars from the half-a-mil in the safe. The look of thanks on the pretty woman's face spoke louder than the words that came out of her mouth.

"I'm glad I didn't have to kill her and that kid."

"Me too Killa," Doc nodded. "Me too"

Chapter 31

"So how was Belize? Did you get over to Manatee Bay? The Blue Hole? Key Caulker?"

"Man, I didn't get nowhere! Didn't get to spend a dime of that money!" Killa laughed a dry humorless laugh. The kind one laughs to avoid crying.

"Why? What happened?" Doc asked sitting up to hear better.

"I got a call. A call that changed both of our lives."

"Grandma!" Killa beamed as his satellite phone rang. The only person who had the untraceable number was his grandmother, who also had one of her own.

"Hey Ma, everything okay?" he asked smiling for his favorite person.

"No, everything is NOT okay!" a strange male voice replied stopping Killa's heart. He checked the caller ID screen to be sure it really was coming from his grandmother's satellite phone. It was.

"A-yo check this," Killa growled in a tone no one has ever heard and lived to tell about. "I don't know how you got this phone, but trust me I will kill everything and everyone you know if anything has happened to my people!"

"Your family is fine. We are only barbarians when we need to be. Your immediate concern should be the property you took from Dallas Dukes," the voice stated so calmly.

Killa looked over to the Duffel bag of money that he had yet to touch from yesterday's robbery. "A-yo, who the fuck are you?"

"You're worried about the wrong thing. Your chief concern is returning The BM's money."

"The BM? His baby mama? Yo, his baby mama blew me right before..."

"The B.M. is The Black Mob! They work for me. That's my money, Dallas was skimming and already on his way to where you sent him, and you will return it!" the voice said finally showing emotion. "You did us a favor, Xavier. Now you work for us, as did your uncle, Cameron Forrest."

"How you know my uncle?" Killa asked, now curious to his core. He knew what his uncle did, now he knew for whom.

"Answer the door and return the money. I'll hold."

"The do...?" Killa said interrupted by a knock on his door. He raised his pistol eye high and snatched it open.

"You don't want to do that," a uniformed police officer said from behind his own raised gun. "The money!"

Killa was so confused his head pounded. How had they found him so quickly? He lowered the gun from the cops face and stepped aside. The officer rushed over and scooped up the bag.

"Here," he said handing Killa a cell phone as he departed with the cash.

"Good, very good," the voice on the phone said as if he could see what was going on. "Now the money you gave to Dallas's woman will be payment for his death.

Congratulations, you now hold the world record for most amount paid for a blow job. Now, go spend some time with that pretty Kitty of yours. We'll be in touch."

The line went dead and Killa immediately called back.

"Xavier? Is everything okay, baby?" his grandmother pleaded fearfully from the off schedule call.

"You tell me. Who's there with you?"

"Just me and Tywa....excuse me, Cameisha. Your uncle and cousin are somewhere in Georgia." Deidra replied.

"Okay," Killa replied still confused. He intended to ask about the new addition to the family but had more pressing matters. "Get rid of the phone, I'll have another one sent."

For the first time, in a very long time, Killa didn't know what to do. The only thing he did know is that he needed more guns. It was time to see Bigs.

****

"How did you get in here?" Big Shawn croaked as Killa appeared in his darkened bedroom.

"I'm getting pretty good at that," Killa chuckled quite pleased with himself. Since he didn't know who was who or who could be trusted he popped in on the dealer without calling. The antiquated security system was a breeze to bypass.

"What do you want?" Bigs asked without moving yet.

"Ice-cream, do you have rocky road?" he replied sarcastically.

"Ice-cream? Nigga I sell guns!"

"Then sell me some guns," Killa smiled. *"And you won't be needing that. Besides, I took the clip out."*

Big Shawn pulled out the small pistol he had been pointing at Killa from under his cover and sure enough it had been unloaded. Killa followed the still shaken gun dealer into the showroom and began to shop.

Big Shawn called out prices that Killa mentally added as he collected different weapons. Then he saw something that scared the hard to scare man.

"WHAT THE FUCK IS THAT?" Killa exclaimed at the sight of the bomb laden vest adorning a mannequin.

"That's um...a special order," Biggs answered reluctantly.

"For who? No, don't tell me." Killa shot back remembering to leave things that didn't concern him alone. After all he was raised in the Bronx, New York aka Mind Yo Business, New York. Imagine how much better the world would be if everyone minded their own business!

Bigs breathed a sigh of relief at not having to tell him the suicide vest was for his uncle. He went on throwing out prices for the guns and explosives Killa collected.

"Oh and this!" Killa nodded approvingly at a huge .50 caliber desert eagle. That came close to the ten grand he had in his pockets. *"We good?"*

"No doubt," Big Shawn shot back. *"Only next time call first and use the door!"*

"That was yesterday. Today I got my first target. They sent it to the phone they gave me along with pictures, an address, and even a personal message from the client to play for the victim before he dies," Killa said sadly.

"Well, what's wrong? Who was it? A woman? A child?" the doctor asked curious by the show of remorse he didn't need his program to decipher.

For a reply Killa tapped his touch screen and pulled up the picture. He doubled checked it again before sliding it across the table to the doctor.

"Me! Who the hell would want to kill me?" he yelled staring at himself on the phone.

"Well, let's see," Killa replied taking the phone back and playing the message that accompanied the hit.

"Hey, you piece of shit!" his ex-father in-law snarled. "We didn't buy that crap about our daughter for one second. Since the police won't act I will. Now, you burn and die! I'll see you in hell!"

"Burn?" Doc asked puzzled.

"Yeah, I'm supposed to burn you and your house to the ground," Killa said sadly.

"Wait! You're not going to do it, you're not going to kill me, are you?"

"Of course not, Doc," Killa sighed to both of their relief. He still hadn't come up with a plan but the doctor had saved his life. He would not kill his friend.

"Well, what are we gonna do? What about your grandmother?" Doc wondered.

"Well, since they want you burned we need a body. They won't know the difference. Do you know any disposable people we can kill?" Killa asked as a plan came together.

"Do I? I know the perfect man for the job!" Doc replied with a snap of his fingers. "As a matter fact, we can kill two birds with one stone. Three even!"

As the doctor made a call to lure his body double to his death Killa rolled another blunt. He had recently decided to quit smoking weed, it just wasn't going to be today. He began channel surfing as Doc spoke.

"Hey, Bob, yes it's me," he began then paused to listen. "That was a long time ago, I'm over it. I have a new life and someone very special in it. That's why I called. I wanted to see if I could pay you a little extra, say ten grand, to come by and touch us both up?"

Doc nodded and listened as his Nemesis took the bait. The plastic surgeon who had been screwing his wife was on the way. He was disposable.

The odd couple was high as a kite laughing hysterically at mating season on *Animal Planet* when the future decedent arrived. Killa slipped into the den as Doc let him in.

"In here," Doc said as the surgeon followed. "Here is your patient."

"Patient?" both Killa and guest asked together.

"That's right, Killa, he's going to give you a face lift. Nothing major, a little off the nose, chin, cheeks, Just enough to beat facial recognition software," Doc explained.

"I don't know what's going on here but I don't like it. I'm leaving!" the surgeon huffed.

"Take one step and it will be your last!" Killa warned.

With no other choice the doctor prepped himself and his patient for the quick procedure. Killa didn't trust the man and refused anesthesia. He grunted once, twice, and then frowned as the doctor rearranged his face. An hour or so after he started he wrapped the killer's face with gauze.

"Stay out of direct sunlight, no showers, and absolutely no touching!" the doctor warned as he pulled off his surgical gloves.

The good doctor was next to go undergo the procedure, took Killa's place in the chair.

"Now, there is just a matter of my pay," the surgeon announced as he finished up on the shrink.

"Here you go!" Doc said as he fired a round into his stomach. The man was confused initially when the gun didn't make any noise. The burning in his gut demanded he run.

Doc was grinning from ear to ear as he followed the man, who surgically enhanced his wife for his own pleasure, shooting as they walked. When he finally fell Doc stood over him and pumped round after round into him before delivering the coup de grâce.

"Wow, that was fun!" he laughed under his bandages. "Gets easier every time. My wife's parents are next."

"No! Next is you disappearing! My life depends on your death, you're now dead! Write a check to him and use his ID to clean out your account."

"I have a retirement fund in San Juan. Guess I'll be retiring a little earlier than planned," Doc sighed.

"Never come back, Doc." Killa warned, the death threat just under the surface of the warning.

As the doctor gathered his traveling supplies Killa got gas cans from the garage. He began by pouring gas directly in the dead man's mouth to make sure that he would never be identified. He poured the remaining two cans around the house making a trail to the front door.

"Well?" Doc asked as they stared at each other in the doorway.

"Well, you're dead, so go live. Me, I've got more killing to do," Killa replied verbally accepting his fate. He was a hired killer now weather he liked it or not.

Both man drove away from the house in different directions but both looked at the orange infernal behind them. Killa's phone began to vibrate and he licked his lips as Kitty's kitty came up on his ID screen.

"I'm on the way," he said answering and closing his phone simultaneously.

The couple fulfilled each other's special request before getting down to an exhausting round of sex. As they basked in the afterglow Kitty turned on the news.

"In breaking news the notorious Cameron Forrest, wanted in connection with the death of five federal agents, was killed today."

"Last night agents raided a night club where Forrest along with reputed New York drug king pin Christopher

Barnes were conducting a deal. An explosion of unknown origin claimed the lives of ten people, three of which were federal agents. Agents Nelson Ford, Adam Landry, and Roland Anderson died during the raid. Some of the bodies have not been identified due to the extent of the fire…"

"You're a dead man!" Killa snarled at the smiling agent taking credit for the death of his uncle.

It took a week to pinpoint the crooked cop's hideaway but only minutes to break in. His surveillance showed the agent should be here just about…

"Hmp?" agent Wilson questioned when the switch failed to illuminate the pitch black room.

"I took the bulb out," Killa announced from across the room in the agent's comfortable recliner.

"For you to be in my house I assume you have a weapon pointed at me?" the agent asked.

"A fucking Canon!" he replied with a laugh, racking the huge pistol as an exclamation point.

"S&W Desert Eagle .50 cal." The weapons expert replied hearing the familiar slide and large round hitting the floor. "My only question is, why are you here?"

"Really?" the intruder laughed.

"Well, to kill me obviously, but why? The world thinks Cameron Forrest is dead. You're good, I'll give you that. We didn't even know about your dad until the DNA came back. I suppressed it, no one knows you're alive. I got a hundred large in my sta…"

"Ninety eight," the gunman corrected letting him know he had the money already.

"So go! Just go, Cam, you won!" Wilson pleaded.

"That sounds like a plan, only I ain't Cam. Don't worry though, the money is for him, a little traveling money," Killa said.

"Who the hell are you then?" Wilson barked, ready to try his luck going for his own gun.

"My name is Xavier," he said hitting the light, "but everyone calls me Killa."

Five rounds from the most powerful handgun on the planet blew chunks out of the crooked cop ruining his plans for the evening and forever.

"Justice!" Killa spat as he looked down on the unholy agent full of holes. He grabbed the sack of dope money and hit the door. He didn't locate the million he had socked away somewhere but he had all the time in the world.

THE END

Epilogue

"What makes you think he'll come here?" Bigs asked yet another uninvited guest. He felt no fear from the man but hated people dropping in on him unannounced.

"Just a hunch," the man replied. "Roll another blunt."

"I'm high as a barrel of oil already!" Bigs complained but complied. He forced another blunt into his system as they waited for someone they weren't sure was coming, then he came.

"Bet a stack that's him," the guest offered as Bigs stood to answer the door bell.

"Bet!" he replied as he made his way to the door. He sucked his teeth at the grand he just lost as he looked through the peephole. As Bigs turned the heavy locks to open the door as his guest stood up to be formally introduced.

"Cam this is Killa. Killa, Cam."

Also available from Sa'id Salaam
*Available in Paperback and E-book

*Killa Season, Chronicles of a Hitman
*Yolo, The Lovely Little Lunatic
*Killa Season 2, The Purge
*Yolo 2, A Beautiful Death
*Yolo 3, Murda Mami
*Sun & Shyne, Growing Pains
Sun & Shyne 2, School Daze
*Sun & Shyne 3, Family Business (pts 2 & 3 are combined
for paperback)

*Dope Boy, The Original
*Dope Girl, (The Girl Who Would Be King)
*Dope Girl 2, Just Like Daddy
*Dope Girl 3, Turn Up
*Dope Girl 4
*Dope Girl 5, The King is Back
*Ra & Dre, A Thugged Out Love Affair
*Ra & Dre, A Thugged Out Love Affair 2
*Ra & Dre, A Thugged Out Love Affair 3
*Ra & Dre, A Thugged Out Love Affair 4

Killa

*Killa Season, Chronicles of a Hitman
*Yolo, The Lovely Little Lunatic
*Killa Season 2, The Purge
*Yolo 2, A Beautiful Death
*Yolo 3, Murda Mami
*Sun & Shyne, Growing Pains
Sun & Shyne 2, School Daze
*Sun & Shyne 3, Family Business (pts 2 & 3 are combined for paperback)
The Champ, Chronicles of a Junky
*The Preacher's Wife, Chronicles of a Junky2
*Lil' Miss Molly, Chronicles of a Junky 3
*White Girl, Chronicles of a Junky 4
*Reverend Cash, Let Us Prey
The Lady Killer
*Yung Pimpin'
*Yung Pimpin' 2
*Love and Hip Hop
*Luv In The Club
*Luv In The Club 2
*Luv In The Club 3
Jack & Ill
The Real Hood Rats of Atlanta
*The Shahadah
*What the Qur'an Says

Coming Soon

218

Sa'id Salaam

Yolo 4, Diary of a Mad Woman
Witches of The West End

Made in the USA
Lexington, KY
21 November 2019